My Life With Wings
And Other Stories

Hal Marcovitz

My Life With Wings
© Hal Marcovitz, 2021. All rights reserved.
ISBN: 979-8-9855065-2-5

All rights reserved. No part of this book may be reproduced or transmitted in any form by any means, electronic or mechanical, including photocopying, recording, or by any information storage and retrieval system, without permission in writing from the copyright owner.

This is a work of fiction. Names, characters, places, and incidents either are the product of the author's imagination or used fictitiously, and any resemblance to any actual persons, living or dead, events, or locales is entirely coincidental.

Cover art by Adefabijo Samuel (with apologies to Guido Reni.)

Covered Bridge Press

My Life With Wings
and Other Stories
Hal Marcovitz

Table of Contents

My Life With Wings	7
Adult Situations, Profanity, Nudity, Sex, Violence	183
Tammy's Tips	199
To Control the Wolf	211
The Spider's Protocol	223

Chapter One

Eggerton discovered the secret room in his attic during the last week of his marriage; he had been poking around in the attic, searching for some paperbacks he found himself hankering to re-read.

When Eggerton pulled some cartons aside, he found a hinged access door, no more than three-feet-square, and when he pulled the access door open, he discovered a small storage room, no more than ten-feet-square. The room was empty; there were no forgotten treasures or hidden caches of pre-Depression banknotes or priceless long-forgotten postage stamp collections, which initially disappointed Eggerton, but his eye was soon drawn to a dormer, and at the end of the dormer, a window.

The house was very old and very tall and Eggerton supposed that during the three years he lived there he had certainly noticed the window from the front yard below, but he had never been sufficiently interested in the window to consider where exactly in the house he could find it.

And so when he crawled through the tiny trap door and stood in the secret attic room, discovering the window, his first thought was: "So that's where that window is. Huh!"

He discovered the window held a magnificent view of the neighborhood. The street on which Eggerton lived was located on a modest hill, and Eggerton's house stood near the very top. So, somebody looking out the window in Eggerton's secret attic room was essentially looking out over the stratosphere. Well, not quite. But you get the idea. Anyway, the window was composed of thick, concave hand-blown panes separated by thin slats of punky wood, all probably dating back to the original construction.

The window opened on a hinge. Eggerton swung open the window and leaned out. Below, he caught sight of a cardinal soaring by. From the window is his secret attic room, Eggerton saw that he was higher than the cardinal flies. He was amused by that. Eggerton suddenly grew wistful and wished he could have made love to his ex-wife Mouse in the secret attic room, and that spontaneous sex on a hard wooden floor would be highly erotic. But that never happened.

Eggerton and Mouse were married three years, seven months and six days. On his first night as a divorced man, Eggerton sat down with pencil, paper and calculator and figured it out. He intended to calculate the length of his marriage to the hour and minute, but quickly decided such a calculation would be impossible because he had no idea what time of day his divorce decree was signed by the judge. He remembered he and Mouse were married at exactly 1:37 in the afternoon because when he was invited to kiss the bride, he discreetly glanced at his watch and made note of the time. But the judge merely dated the divorce decree. Which was fine with Eggerton. He was glad Mouse was out of his life. Often, he wondered how they lasted together three years, seven months and six days.

The terms of the divorce were settled quickly: the house along with its mortgage would go to Eggerton; Mouse would receive everything else—bank accounts, mutual fund accounts, money market accounts, stocks, bonds, the works. Mouse, through her attorney, made it very clear on the issue of the house: she did not wish to be stuck with a bad debt following a bad marriage. Which was fine with Eggerton.

Buying the house had been the one decision he made with Mouse he didn't regret. Shortly after meeting with Mouse's lawyer for the amicable distribution meeting (that term made Eggerton laugh), Eggerton sat down with pencil, paper and calculator and figured out that he and Mouse bought the house after having been married two years, four months and seven days. Again, nobody recorded the hour and minute when the papers were signed at the settlement table.

Eggerton concluded that in the future, when the next big moment occurs in his life, he would mark down the time...to the second. Out of habit, he glanced at his watch. Nearly 4 o'clock in the morning. He was beginning to feel drowsy. Soon, to bed. Soon, to bed...alone.

Eggerton hadn't slept with a woman since Mouse moved out a year ago. He found himself far less interested in dating than he thought he would be. On his first night alone in the house, Eggerton fell asleep in front of the TV; he awoke in a clammy summertime shiver at 5 o'clock in the morning, the dismal glow of a wry BBC comedy blurring his face. He blinked hard, slipped out of his clothes and went to bed. And then he slept long into the afternoon.

The house has four bedrooms. Eggerton insisted on a four-bedroom house because he wanted children. Mouse said she wanted children, too, but Eggerton doubted that she was ever really serious about wanting to be a mother.

Still, she went along with him on buying a four-bedroom house, and Eggerton was grateful for that. Eggerton couldn't recall Mouse ever agreeing with him again.

The house was built in the 1920s. It had a tiny backyard, but Eggerton added a patio made out of burnt-orange terra cotta tiles and tasteful, knee-high evergreen landscaping around the patio, and then, finally, one of those Cinzano tables on top of the patio and, in the final analysis, it was all really quite elegant. Eggerton enjoyed sitting on the patio, sipping coffee and reading novels. He bought one of those boombox CD players and would take it onto the patio with him and play jazz. Eggerton's favorite artist was Charlie Parker, the saxophone player. Bird, they called him. Sometimes, on warm and lazy Sundays, he would plant himself at the Cinzano table shortly after lunch and read and drink coffee and listen to Bird Parker on the CD player the entire day, getting up and going into the house only to pee.

VOYAGE A LA LUNE.

Chapter Two

Eggerton worked as a copy editor at a newspaper. He enjoyed the work and the hours. His work day started 6 o'clock at night and ended 2 o'clock in the morning. Then, he would go home and sleep. He'd rise before noon and spend the day in the house or, if the weather was warm, on the terra cotta patio reading and drinking coffee. Eggerton enjoyed black coffee and wasn't bothered by the caffeine. At work, his job required him to dummy in the long and redundant lists of stock and bond prices, the NASDAQ quotes, the mutual fund listings, the NYSE, the Dow, the S&P, the Treasuries, the futures, and the various and sundry other investments followed closely and religiously by people with money, gobs and gobs of money, all printed in eye-numbing agate type, stacked alongside one another in deadly tombstone-style grey columns.

Eggerton's job was to make everything fit nicely on the broadsheet pages of the newspaper. This he did with aplomb; indeed, he was proud of his stock and bond listings, regarding them as the true heart and soul of the newspaper. It was easy work and paid well and he had no ambition to move up the ladder into management. He also turned down many opportunities to switch to day hours. He much preferred his labors over the stock and bond tables to routine copy editing—the dismal chore practiced by his peers that required them to read and correct the grammar and punctuation in the stories written by the newspaper's reporters. They found themselves constantly in confrontations with the reporters, who were disdainful of all efforts to improve their journalism. Eggerton could live without the confrontational aspects of the job, no question about that.

Occasionally, Eggerton would accompany the other copy editors for drinks after work. He didn't go too often because their conversations bored him. They insisted on talking shop and criticizing reporters, whom they regarded as fools and crybabies. Eggerton would go to the bar to be a good sport, but he would be repulsed by everyone's drunkenness and soon find excuses to leave.

"Well, gotta go. Meeting somebody," he would say.

"Later," they would say.

Eggerton would nod his head.

"Yeah, later," he would say.

And then he would leave the bar and go home. Sometimes, during the summer, if he were not tired when he arrived home, Eggerton would brew a pot of coffee and sit on his terra cotta deck, reading under a porch light until sunrise. Then, he would watch the new sun splash vivid and comforting colors across his backyard. He enjoyed that. Finally, feeling drowsy, he would make his way upstairs and sleep the rest of the day.

Although he resisted dating and preferred not to mingle with coworkers, Eggerton still had many friends. He saw them often, enjoyed their company and regarded himself as far from lonely. His friends would often egg him on, offering to find him dates with eligible women they knew, but Eggerton would have none of it. He told them he would start seeing women again when he felt the time was right.

Most of his friends were single. During their marriage, Eggerton and Mouse did not try to nurture friendships with other married couples. Mostly, they found themselves spending time with the friends they had before they were married, most of whom managed to stay single during those years.

My Life With Wings

After he broke up with Mouse, Eggerton continued to hang around with his single friends. He was, after all, single again himself. Eggerton supposed that if Mouse had become pregnant they would have spent time with other couples expecting babies, but that never happened.

One of Eggerton's friends was Crane, whom he had known since high school. Crane lived close by, but they didn't see each other more than once or so a week because Crane worked days.

Crane was employed as a physical therapist at a hospital. He was tall, lanky as a stork and skinnier than Eggerton. Crane had a shock of red hair that tended to curl when he let it grow long, which he occasionally did, wearing his hair in a ponytail. Recently, he had also let the hair on his chin grow, but Crane's facial hair came in as a downy fuzz, which didn't lend itself to forming a proper beard. Still, Crane liked the look. He often told himself, as he primped in front of his mirror in the morning, that his beard made him look special.

"Oh. . .so. . .special," Crane would sing to himself.

He was a very good physical therapist, having won the Physical Therapist of the Year Award at the hospital in three out of the last seven years. Each time he won, Crane attended a banquet where the hospital administrator presented him with a shellacked oak-veneer-on-particle-board plaque with his name inscribed in a fake bronze plate below the words "Physical Therapist of the Year." And below the name of the winner, the plaque manufacturer included a tiny etched-in-fake-bronze rendering of a human being, depicted from shoulders to head, the subject's muscular system exposed, with the subject's sterno-cleido-mastoid muscle highlighted in bas relief.

It was an excellent rendering of an exposed muscular system and, in fact, the design won the manufacturer and his staff artist top awards at the International Exposition of Award, Trophy and Plaque Manufacturers, which meets for a weekend every August at the MGM Grand in Las Vegas.

The sterno-cleido-mastoid is, by the way, a muscle in the human neck. Physical therapists often have to manipulate the sterno-cleido-mastoid in patients suffering from neck distress. The presence of the sterno-cleido-mastoid etching on the plaque had given the award a bit of a personality, and among the physical therapists at the hospital the Physical

Therapist of the Year Award had become known, in their jargon, as the Sterno Cleido Award, or, more familiarly, the Sternie.

In any event, Crane owned three Sternies. Crane was very proud of the plaques, and delightfully hung them in his apartment. He chose a wall for their display that had plenty of room left over for future Sternies. Crane was also very proud of the white uniform issued by the hospital, and would leave it on long after his workday had concluded.

Surreptitiously, Crane kept an extra pair of white uniform slacks in his locker at work. On one occasion, Crane used the lav and neglected to shake the final few drops of urine from Ol' Finchie (Crane's nickname for his pecker) and, some hours later, was horrified to notice two dried and yellow urine stains on his trousers. He wondered if anyone had noticed. He discovered the stains about two hours before his shift ended and, while holding a sheaf of papers over his crotch, reported to his supervisor that he was feeling ill and would like to go home early. At home, Crane tossed out the trousers, believing they were indelibly stained. In any event, to prevent a similar mishap, Crane always shook Ol' Finchie five times at the urinal (counting out loud, regardless of whoever else may have been occupying the neighboring urinal.)

At home, he practiced self-control by performing kegel exercises each night before bed and each morning before leaving for work, believing that stronger pelvic muscles would reduce his need to urinate (under the theory that if he could suppress the urge to pass his water, he would not expose himself to the danger of staining the crotch of his white pants with urine drops.) And, finally, he did have the extra pair of white uniform pants in his locker in case the unthinkable would occur again. So, when it came to guarding against unwanted urine stains on his pants, Crane felt he had prepared for any and all eventualities.

Crane harbored an equal admiration for the other parts of his uniform as well. On the pocket of his white shirt, the name "Crane" was neatly stitched in red thread in a cursive style. Crane often marveled at the skill of the seamstress who sewed his name on his uniform shirt. Although it wasn't required, Crane wore white shoes and white socks with his white uniform. Crane thought he looked oh-so-special in white.

Eggerton saw Woody a bit more often, although he lived across the city. Woody worked nights. He was the night manager of a fast-food restaurant that specialized in spicy Buffalo wings. The name of the restaurant was the Happy Buffalo Wing, and everybody who worked there had to wear white cotton hats with little yellow wings jutting off from the sides, similar to the headgear worn by the comic book hero the Flash, whose headgear was intended to mimic the helmet worn by the Roman god Mercury. There was nothing, well, flashy, about the hats worn by the employees of the 347 nationally franchised Happy Buffalo Wing restaurants. The hat worn by a Happy Buffalo Wing employee looked like the black-billed and flat-topped kepi-style hat you might see on the head of a French Foreign Legionnaire only, of course, a Legionnaire would never be found traipsing through the desert with a winged hat. Also, on the front of the hat, a broad, toothy smile was embroidered. Hence, proof that Buffalo wings are happy. The Madison Avenue-based advertising agency retained by the Happy Buffalo Wing corporate office (in Birdsboro, Pennsylvania) came up with the design for the hat, and featured singing and dancing actors wearing the winged kepis in all Happy Buffalo Wing commercials. Most of the commercials also featured a few bars from the Happy Buffalo Wing's theme song, which was "Shuffle Off to Buffalo," a decidedly old song; nevertheless, the rights of which were made available to the company for a surprisingly modest fee. As for Woody, he wore the hat as much as possible because he was going bald and it helped cover up his shiny pate, which tended to sweat and reflect the migraine-inducing green-tinted fluorescence from the overhead lights in the restaurant.

Woody often didn't leave work until after midnight. Eggerton and Woody enjoyed taking late meals together. Woody was twice-divorced and lived alone, too. Woody was incredibly corpulent: he weighed close to 300 pounds, and would waddle like a penguin when he walked. Probably, his waddle was due to his arthritic knees, which hurt him very much. Nevertheless, he steadfastly refused his doctor's admonitions to lose weight, which Woody was told would make his knees feel better. Woody had trouble keeping the top button of his shirt buttoned. He also had trouble keeping the bottom buttoned as well; usually, Eggerton could see Woody's navel jutting out of his shirt. He tried not to look, feeling himself mildly repulsed at the site of Woody's hairy umbilicus. Still, Eggerton found Woody good company. He had a high, squeaky laugh that was genuinely infectious, and Eggerton rarely found him in a dour mood. He liked Woody and wished he could spend more time with him.

Eggerton had a good friend named Martin. Martin used to work as a copy editor at the newspaper, but quit to become a novelist. Martin never sold a novel, but he did manage to scratch out a living writing freelance magazine articles. Some months ago, Martin was hired by a medical journal to write a story about Bashful Bladder Syndrome. Men who suffer from Bashful Bladder Syndrome are unable to urinate in public restrooms due, mostly, to psychological barriers that seal off the urethra like chewing gum blown through a soda straw—a mental gonorrhea, essentially.

Martin wrote 5,000 words about Bashful Bladder Syndrome and realized that he had only just scratched the surface of this intriguing malady. After Martin finished the story, he decided to see if he could expand the article into a book. So, he wrote an outline and sent it to a number of publishers and, indeed, a publisher of hastily-authored and not always accurate consumer medical guides did write back to Martin willing to publish his book about Bashful Bladder Syndrome and offering an advance of $1,000, which Martin quickly accepted. Martin proposed to name the book *The Timid Tinkler*, but the publisher didn't think that would be a good idea and preferred, instead, the simpler yet self-evident title of *Bashful Bladder Syndrome*.

Nevertheless, Martin was hard at work on the project, which often required him to hang around public restrooms where he attempted to interview men who seemed to have an unnatural hesitancy while urinating as he watched. Several times, he was questioned by park policemen and mall security officers who seldom believed his story about researching a book about overly resistant bladders, and was asked to leave the park or the mall, which Martin always did with haste because he certainly didn't want to risk arrest or a fine over the matter. There were plenty of parks and malls with public restrooms, and Martin was confident that he would soon obtain the requisite number of interviews with true sufferers of Bashful Bladder Syndrome. At the present time, three BBS sufferers had agreed to be interviewed, although none of them would allow Martin to use their real names. (One fellow, a timid tinkler named

Griffin, did consent to the use of his first name, which Martin regarded as genuine progress in the preparation of the manuscript.)

Martin always dressed impeccably—suits, dress shoes, silk ties, the works, but he did let his hair down from time to time, and enjoyed wearing casual khaki pants and Hawaiian shirts and unshined shoes without socks.

Kiwi was another friend. Kiwi dated Eggerton before Eggerton met Mouse. Kiwi had a government job; she worked in the prothonotary's office in city hall. Kiwi typed labels for file folders. She majored in literature in college and wrote her thesis on Harper Lee. After college she couldn't find work as a literature teacher but her uncle knew the prothonotary and talked to him, and that's how Kiwi landed the job. She had been typing labels in the prothonotary's office for five years when she met Eggerton.

Kiwi and Eggerton slept together a dozen times before Kiwi broke it off. At first, Kiwi and Eggerton had little in common except physical attraction. Kiwi had wide, saucer-shaped brown eyes, an oval face and a tightly-cropped haircut that neatly framed her features. She wore rimless granny glasses (her vision was rather poor) and long cotton skirts without stockings, and she was partial to sandals which meant she often had dirty toes. Eggerton noticed that her toes were usually quite grimy but, for reasons he couldn't explain to himself, found them highly sensual. Kiwi liked to smoke marijuana; Eggerton did not. When Kiwi smoked grass, she would soar like an eagle and then get silly and laugh at Eggerton's jokes. During sex, Kiwi insisted on sitting atop Eggerton, striding him horse-on-rider style, where she thrashed around and wailed, swinging her arms wildly while making whooping sounds. She also insisted on wearing her granny glasses during sex, which Eggerton found unusual, and when, after he had exploded inside her and she collapsed on top of him, he noticed that her granny glasses were steamed up and she couldn't see out of them for several minutes, until the condensation gradually disappeared. Still, Kiwi had her serious side and could be moody. During those times, Eggerton and Kiwi had trouble talking with one another, and when Kiwi told Eggerton she wanted to break off their relationship he couldn't say he hadn't see it coming, although he was enormously disappointed. They remained friends, though, and would often check in with each other from time to time and occasionally meet for drinks. Looking back on their relationship, Eggerton concluded that Kiwi would have really gone for a spontaneous screw on the hard wooden floor of the secret room in his attic. She was the type who would. But that never happened.

Eggerton met Mouse at a party given by Crane. Eggerton prefers to bring dates to Crane's parties, because Crane has a lot of friends who are physical therapists and they often corner Eggerton and insist on discussing strained ligaments or pulled groins or sprains or arthritic discs. He very politely listens and nods knowingly, not wanting to be rude but, nevertheless, is bored by their constant prattle. It is much easier to simply walk into the party with a girlfriend and hold her hand for a good fifteen or twenty minutes and talk in a very audible tone about films or books or stories in the news until everyone in the place catches onto the message you are not into physical therapy chatter.

This time, though, Eggerton's date backed out at the last minute—the flu, she said...yeah, the flu, said Eggerton—and Eggerton found himself going on his own. He briefly considered staying home, but Crane was his friend and he promised to go so he went without Lazuli, which was the queer yet true and accurate name of the flu sufferer. That night, after enduring several vigorous discussions about anterior and posterior crucial ligaments, he met Mouse. They talked. Eggerton told her he worked as a copy editor at a newspaper, although he didn't think she understood what the job was all about. She told Eggerton her name is Mouse and when Eggerton asked her how she acquired her name, she said she didn't remember, that when she was a kid her older sisters started calling her Mouse because, Mouse supposed, she was the youngest and smallest in the family and Mouse is the type of name youngest and smallest people typically find themselves being called. Anyway, Mouse said, her real name is Mary Anne but nobody ever calls her Mary Anne, everybody calls her Mouse.

Mouse told Eggerton she enjoys music; Eggerton asked her what kind. She mentioned some rock groups that Eggerton had never heard of. He said, "Oh, yeah; right, them." He was sure she couldn't tell he was faking. That night, she wore a heavy dose of too-sweet perfume, which Eggerton found pungent, but kept his mouth shut about that because he sincerely wanted to sleep with her. Later that evening, Eggerton got Mouse drunk and took her to his apartment, where they had sex. Soon, Mouse moved in with him and then they married and bought the house and then divorced, and Eggerton was certain Mouse was screwing other guys but he never asked her about it because he was, after all, screwing other women.

One of his girlfriends was Rhea, a copy editor. Rhea made up the sports pages. Rhea was divorced and slightly overweight, which is an occupational hazard for copy editors because they do a lot of sitting and very few of them take the time to exercise, and a lot of them eat high-fat iced pastries dispensed from vending machines. A lot of copy editors have bad teeth, too. Eggerton, however, is not overweight and does not have bad teeth. He is rail-thin with a bony ass and ribs that stretch through his skin like the spokes of a bicycle wheel. Eggerton tries to watch his diet and makes it a habit to brush his teeth often. Anyway, one time after work, Eggerton, Rhea and some of the other copy editors went out for drinks. Rhea got very drunk that night. Eggerton drove her home. She invited him up for a nightcap and Eggerton surprised himself by saying "Well, OK." Upstairs, Rhea poured Eggerton a glass of wine and then sat down beside him. They talked briefly and nervously, and Eggerton knew it was up to him, so he advanced on her, dismissing his final fleeting thought of his wife Mouse, and Rhea pulled him in deeply. After that, Eggerton and Rhea slept together occasionally; usually, at her invitation. Eggerton obliged Rhea, even though he was still married to Mouse. He knew it was wrong but he did it anyway.

But for the last year, ever since Mouse walked out on him, Eggerton had little interest in sex and dating. Whenever Rhea would call or suggest at work that he come by for drinks later, he would always make excuses. The time, he assured himself, just wasn't right. When the time would be right, he wasn't sure.

Chapter Three

It was just past 4 o'clock in the morning. Eggerton had been sitting at the kitchen table, sipping black coffee and playing soft jazz on a CD player, but now he put down his novel and walked up the stairs to his bedroom. He was drowsy. He brushed his teeth and stripped off his clothes, leaving on his boxer shorts, only. The boxer shorts were decorated with comically large black and white vertical stripes. Mouse bought him the shorts as a birthday present a year ago, more as a gag gift than as a serious article of clothing. Oddly, though, he found the shorts very comfortable and enjoyed wearing them. And besides, it was a warm evening and Eggerton hated air-conditioning, running the window box in his bedroom on the most oppressive nights, only. And so, the black-and-white striped boxer shorts suited him perfectly for the night ahead.

He fell asleep quickly, although his last memory before dozing off was of a mild but by no means distracting ache between his shoulder blades. He dreamed of having sex with a voluptuous lingerie model who appeared in an advertisement that ran for a week on the pages that included the New York Stock Exchange listings. Eggerton considered it a curious place in the newspaper to find an advertisement for lingerie, but he gave the matter no further thought—other than his subconscious desire to have sex with the model.

Eggerton woke up close to noon. He found himself sleeping on his stomach, which was odd. He didn't enjoy sleeping that way and felt out of sorts. He sat up, stretched his arms over his head and then walked into the bathroom to pee. As he turned away from the toilet, he caught a glimpse of himself in the bathroom mirror.

Eggerton noticed that, overnight, he had grown wings.

He was startled. He stepped back from the mirror, closed his eyes tightly, then reopened them and regarded himself. His image had not changed. He still had wings.

He briefly recalled his dream of having sex with the lingerie model and wondered whether the dream included a sexual encounter in mid-air and that, somehow, this vision remained in his mind even after waking up. He allowed himself a brief smile. "Boy," he thought to himself, "that would have been a great experience—doing it in free-fall." After giving it no more than a second or two of thought, though, he concluded that— to the best of recollection— his most recent dream did not include free-fall intercourse and, therefore, there was no reason to carry a mental image of winged coitus into real life.

Indeed, he found himself gazing in the mirror again and saw the two feathery wings that were spreading out behind his reflection were, in fact, very, very real. There was no longer any doubt in his mind. Yes, he had somehow grown wings.

He regarded them closely. They were broad, auburn-and-coppery feathered wings stemming from his inner shoulders. They hung nearly to his heels. Perhaps it was a gag. Had one of his friends broken in at night with a pair of phony, costume-store wings and glued them to his back?

He turned away from the mirror, craned his neck over his shoulder, and examined his back. No, these weren't glued on. He could plainly see the junction of the wings to his back, how the skin metamorphosed into the two new appendages growing out of his body.

My Life With Wings

Eggerton closed the lid of the toilet and sat down to think it over. He found himself arranging his wings behind his back so he could settle his rump on the toilet lid. His new wings were awkward and Eggerton suspected he would have to learn new ways to move his body in relation to the physical world. It took a few seconds, but he eventually found a way to sit comfotably on the toilet lid.

But then he jumped to his feet, looked quickly around, and started dashing about the house. It took a few minutes but, finally, he found a pencil and returned to the bathroom. Once again, he sat down on the toilet lid. He took a paper napkin from the dispenser on the vanity. It was pink and decorated at the four corners by tiny flowers embossed in bas relief images. Mouse bought the napkins before the divorce and they had remained in the vanity dispenser. There were still napkins in the vanity dispenser because Eggerton was usually not prone to using them. In most cases, he wiped his hands on his shirt or pants.

Eggerton pondered the napkin for a moment and made a mental note to replace the napkins with something a bit more plain—perhaps napkins that were tan or brown, an earthen color would be nice.

But back to the task at hand. He concluded that he had to use a prissy bas relief napkin for this very important task because a sheet of toilet paper would never work—much too thin for penmanship. He glanced at his watch and wrote: "12:02 p.m. and 27 seconds, noticed I have wings." He placed the napkin neatly on top of the vanity and made a mental note to retrieve it later and enter the date and time properly in some sort of log, the nature of which he had yet to conceive.

That done, Eggerton decided to give this whole curious episode the thought he knew it deserved.

Chapter Four

Eggerton decided to tell other people. First, he would have to tell the newspaper—although he wasn't sure exactly what story he would give them. He was, after all, due to arrive at work in five hours or so. For now, he concluded it would be easiest to call in sick. So, he called the newspaper and talked to the day city editor. He told the day city editor he didn't feel well and wouldn't be in that night and that he should pass the message on to the night city editor, who would have to assign the stock and bond listings to another copy editor. The day city editor grunted an acknowledgement and said he would, but never told Eggerton he hoped he would recover and return soon in good health.

Actually, Eggerton was grateful for the day city editor's disinterest in his well-being. If the editor had, in fact, asked him the nature of his malady, what was he to say? Feathers? Obviously, that response would prompt further questions.

And so, before he called Eggerton concocted a clever cover story: If asked, Eggerton resolved, he would tell the day city editor that he caught a cold. Yes, a cold was good. It would do. He even practiced a fake cough and fake sneeze before he made the call.

"Cufff," Eggerton rasped, looking at his image in the bathroom mirror to see if the fake cough seemded genuine.

"Chooo," he said next.

He concluded that the fake cough sounded more genuine than the fake sneeze, but to successfully pull off the act he would have to offer both—the cufff and the chooo.

He decided that when he called in sick if he detected any notion of doubt in the day city editor's response to his reported illness, Eggerton would react with the fake cough and then, after a pause of a few seconds, the fake sneeze. After practicing his fake coughs and sneezes several times, Eggerton was sure he could pull off the ruse.

And yet, a seed of doubt remained buried deep in his subconscious because Eggerton had never been a particularly effective liar. And so, when he finally made the call he felt a bit anxious as he reported his illness to the day city editor but the day city editor seemed to accept Eggerton's story and, therefore, was saved from having to perform his fake cough and sneeze.

Next, he decided to call Crane. He knew Crane would still be at work and hoped he could catch him between patients.

Eggerton was in luck. Crane took the call.

"Can you come over?" he asked Crane.

"When? After work?"

"Uhh, yeah. Uhh, as soon as you can, really," said Eggerton.

Crane suspected his friend was in some sort of trouble. He could tell from the tone of his voice. Crane was good that way. Crane told Eggerton that he sounded a bit, well, desperate.

"I am," said Eggerton.

"Tell me what's wrong."

There was a pause on the phone.

"I can't," said Eggerton.

Another pause.

"Come on," Crane said. "Tell Ol' Cranie."

Crane often liked to refer to himself as Ol' Cranie. Eggerton had no idea why. Occasionally, Crane would also call himself "The Cranester" and even, when helped along by liquor, "The Cranemaster General." Eggerton thought Crane could be silly at times.

"Well?" Crane said. "What's the problem?"

Eggerton said he couldn't talk about it. Crane said he was busy after work, but he would re-arrange things and see if he could make it over. It was a lie, of course. Crane had no plans. Before Eggerton called, Crane intended to go to a bar downtown and seek a partner for casual sex.

Which Crane was quite adept at finding whenever he felt the urge, which was quite often. Crane had a relaxed and easy personality. He was good at making people feel comfortable, which he found worked very well with women he met in bars. Women were, after all, showing up in those bars for the same reason as Crane—to hopefully partner-up with an attractive stranger. But many women were wary, of course. Crane was very good at recognizing this trait and using his easygoing, relaxed personality to put the women he met at ease and, in many cases, find his way into their beds later in the evening.

But Eggerton was a friend in need and Crane decided he could delay his bar-hopping routine that evening.

"I'll be over after work," Crane said.

Eggerton said that would be fine, he'd wait for him.

"Surgery," Crane told him, after he arrived at Eggerton's house, let himself in, took a bottle of beer out of Eggerton's refrigerator, saw that his friend had wings and responded to Eggerton's question as to what he should do next.

Eggerton raised his eyebrows.

"You mean I should go to a doctor and have them amputated?"

"That's how The Cranester sees it," The Cranester said.

Crane was, in fact, happy that Eggerton asked him what to do. It gave him the opportunity to suggest a medical solution. As a physical therapist, Crane regarded the practice of medicine with the serious tone he knew it deserved.

Eggerton said he'd have to think it over.

Crane was hungry. He asked Eggerton whether he had anything to eat. No, Eggerton said. He hadn't had a chance to go to the market. In fact, Eggerton noticed that he was hungry as well. He hadn't eaten since he woke up shortly before noon and noticed he had grown wings. Now, his hunger caught up with him and he suddenly very much wanted to eat. He asked Crane if he would mind going to the store for some groceries. Eggerton said he wouldn't feel right, you know, going out with wings. Crane said he understood and would do anything to help his friend. Eggerton gave Crane $40. Crane went to the market, spent just under $33 and kept the $7 and change left over. He thought he earned it for making the trip. Eggerton never did ask for change.

Crane made sandwiches of cold cuts, lettuce, onions and cheese, which they ate in the kitchen. Eggerton would have preferred to eat al fresco on the terra cotta patio, but he worried about being spotted by the neighbors. As for Crane, he reached into a jar of dill pickles he picked up at the market. He withdrew a pickle with his fingers and ate it like a carrot, making crunching sounds as he chewed. Eggerton ate as well, although a bit more silently.

"Want me to ask around the hospital? You know, which doctors specialize in amputations?" Crane asked, wiping the pickle juice from his fingers on a napkin. Crane was still wearing his white physical therapy uniform and wouldn't think of wiping his fingers on his pants.

Eggerton sipped his beer. Maybe, Eggerton said, it wouldn't hurt to collect some names. Crane said he would do that. By now, Crane was growing bored. He wanted to help his friend but there was, in all honesty, nothing more that he could do other than make suggestions.

He still hoped to make it to a pub that night. He had a place named the Owl's Nest in mind. It wasn't too far from Eggerton's house. He could be there in minutes.

He selected another pickle from the jar, judged it edible based mostly on its heft, said he would ask a few doctors if they did that type of work, told Eggerton to leave things to Ol' Cranie, let himself out, went to a bar, and eventually used Eggerton's $7 and change to buy a drink for a 21-year-old physical therapy student named Daphne. She was from England. Everybody called her Duckie.

Crane was immediately drawn to Duckie because he saw she was still wearing her white physical therapy uniform. She was slim and small-breasted, which Crane found attractive. Her bobbed hair was jet black, which when contrasted against her white uniform exuded a sensuality Crane found irresistible. In addition to a white uniform she wore white shoes and white stockings. She confided to him that white shoes and stockings were not required by the school, but she enoyed wearing white clothes. Of course, The Cranester turned on his charm and placed Duckie completely at ease. They enjoyed their time together in the bar, mostly sharing their ideas about the art and techniques of physical therapy. Later, at his apartment, Crane took off Duckie's white stockings with his teeth.

Chapter Five

An exchange of emails...

To: HShrike@columbarymedicalcenter.com
From: DBullfinch@columbarymedicalcenter.com

Hank, I thought you'd want to know about an unusual request I received today. One of the hospital's physical therapists—I believe his name is Kane—asked my receptionist if I would provide an amputation for a friend. She told him our patients are typically referred to us by other doctors who have examined the patients and detected a need for surgery.

She asked Mr. Kane what kind of amputation his friend had in mind and he told her the fellow needs his wings cut off.

Neither my receptionist nor I are clear on what exactly Mr. Kane may have meant by that. Nevertheless, she said Mr. Kane was quite serious and she took the question at face value. In any event, I feel Mr. Kane bears watching. I thought you'd want to know. How's your golf game? Still making those birdies?

Doug.

To: DBullfinch@columbarymedicalcenter.com
From: HShrike@columbarymedicalcenter.com

Doug, you are the third surgeon to tell me about this guy who, by the way, is named Crane, not Kane. Anyway, I looked at the guy's work record and he seems pretty straight—he won the Sternie last year.

So, right now I don't think any other action is necessary. But if he asks about his friend with wings again, let me know.

Shot a birdie on a par 5 last week.

Hank.

To: HShrike@columbarymedicalcenter.com
From: DBullfinch@columbarymedicalcenter.com

Hank: That guy Kane came around again. He asked my receptionist if she had spoken with me about providing an amputation for his friend. Again, he insisted that his friend needs his wings cut off. I'm not kidding. I think it's time somebody speaks with Kane to find out what's going on here.

You should have seen me on the course yesterday. I was really killing it. I nailed a birdie on the third hole—you know, that real tricky bastard with the bunker in front of the green.

And then, I came oh-so-close to an eagle on that short par 4 fifth hole. I placed my drive in the center of the fairway, about 120 yards from the pin. My second shot hit the green and rolled right up to the pin, stopping just six inches short of the cup. I settled for the birdie but an eagle would have been something special.

My Life With Wings

Anyway, let me know if you talk to this guy Kane. He is really annoying, although my receptionist seems a bit smitten with him. She says he is rather charming and she hopes he asks her out on a date. She also told me she felt sorry for his friend—you know, the guy with wings.

Doug

Chapter Six

Eggerton spent a sleepless night. He stayed up late reading—which he was forced to do while sitting on a backless stool in the kitchen, which he found terribly uncomfortable. He did find himself growing drowsy, but when he retired to bed he was unable to sleep. He just couldn't find comfort in bed. He was forced to sleep on his stomach, which he found impossible. He really had to labor to breathe. Sleeping on his back, which he preferred, was, of course, out of the question. He tried sleeping on his side, but that didn't work, either. The damned wings kept getting in the way, and he found it quite painful whenever he rolled over on them.

So, at about 6 o'clock in the morning—well early for Eggerton's internal clock—he rose and wandered about the house. He would have preferred to sit on the terra cotta patio and sip coffee during sunrise, but Eggerton didn't want to risk being seen by the neighbors. No, he must stay indoors for now. But for how long? Eggerton shuddered. He simply didn't have an answer.

For reasons he couldn't explain, Eggerton found himself drawn to the attic, where he sat on cartons of his ex-wife's old clothes, which she never bothered to take with her when she moved out. He breathed in heavily, drawing in the dusty, dry air of the attic, and found that it made him lightheaded, so he was careful to take short, measured breaths. Eggerton picked up some old *National Geographic* magazines he owned since he was a kid. He started absently paging through them. Soon, his eye fell on a story. It had something to do with the loons of Minnesota. The story read:

> *Molting wing feathers give the adult loon a somewhat scruffy appearance in winter but are a healthy sign of the bird's upcoming spring migration northward. Ungainly and awkward on turf, loons are marvelously built for water. With relatively small wings, they seem like feathered seals underwater, where they twist, turn, and pivot faster than most fish, their chief prey. Their powerful legs are completely enclosed in their body; only ankles and feet protrude. Heavy bones, not honeycombed with air sacs as most bird bones are, further equip them to be agile divers and strong underwater swimmers. Loons rely on superb eyes to locate their food and pursue it underwater. Prowling for fish, a loon slightly submerges its head and slowly turns it from side to side to look deep into the water in a unique behavior termed peering.*

He sat silently for a few minutes, staring at the colorful Kodachrome images of Minnesota's loons—noble birds, he thought, and not at all ...well, loony. He found himself strangely envious of them.

He read on about the loons but eventually grew bored. Eggerton noticed the tiny trap door for the secret room. He opened it, and found that he could just barely slip through by pulling his wings tightly into his back. Since growing wings, Eggerton found he could control them to some extent by flexing the infraspinatus and supraspinatus muscles in his upper back. He was, in fact, becoming quite adept at manipulating his wings through trapeziusian muscle movements. He made a mental note to ask Crane about this new-found ability; indeed, he was certain his friend would find it interesting.

My Life With Wings

Eggerton stood in the empty room and took inventory of himself. He was still wearing the same black and white striped boxer shorts that he had been wearing the previous morning when he discovered his wings. He had eaten just one meal—the sandwich Crane made the evening before—and yet he wasn't terribly hungry. He needed a shave. He hadn't bathed in two days and could detect his own body odor. He thought about taking a shower and ruled it out, and didn't think he could sit in a bathtub, either. A sponge bath? That would work. He made a mental note to take a sponge bath later in the morning.

Eggerton caught sight of the window in the attic room. The window faced east, and it was just catching the sun as it rose gleaming in the morning sky. A yellow ray of sunshine poured in, and Eggerton noticed the suspended particles of dust drifting in the shaft of light. He walked over to the window and let his body break the plane of sunlight. The heat from the early morning sun felt refreshing on his bare chest. He found himself perspiring under the arms. He raised his arms to the sunlight to help dry out his armpits and stretch his muscles in the warmth. Behind him, he could feel his wings expand. By now, the sunlight was flooding all around Eggerton. He felt more refreshed now than he had been since before this wings thing began. He did some neck rolls to help stretch his spine.

While rolling his head over his shoulders, he noticed an odd shadow behind him. Still facing the window, he turned his head to look. And there, behind him on the floor of the secret attic room, Eggerton saw the shadow of his body, and was surprised to see his wings spread out to their full majestic grandeur, as though he were an eagle posing for his portrait on the back of the dollar bill.

Chapter Seven

Eggerton decided he would require a cot. An Army cot. One made of canvas stretched over wooden rails that could be folded up and packed away until needed. Of course, Eggerton would have no need to fold the cot. He would set it up in the secret attic room and sleep there.

On his stomach, to be sure, but Eggerton believed he would have a good night's sleep if he could sleep on an Army cot. Eggerton thought he might be able to find such a cot in one of those Army-Navy surplus stores. He knew where there was such a store—not more than two blocks from the newspaper. It was named Clyde's Army-Navy Surplus Store.

He had been in there once because he saw a coupon from the store in the newspaper offering Army surplus pea-green T-shirts for half price. As with the lingerie ad, Eggerton regarded it as odd that Clyde, the supposed proprietor, requested his coupon published on the stock market tables pages—an area of the newspaper one hardly associated with armed services surplus shoppers—but Eggerton never considered the matter worth taking up with the advertising salesman who handled Clyde's account. Nevertheless, Eggerton thought Clyde's offer regarding the T-shirts was a good deal, and since he was prone to wearing T-shirts while sipping coffee and reading novels on his terra cotta patio, he decided to, well, have a look-see.

Inside Clyde's, he found a cluttered emporium with narrow aisles, choked with all manner of military gewgaws and accessories, such as empty cartridge belts and vests with pouches that dangled from the armpits and camouflaged covers for tank helmets and canteens complete with their rough fabric holders and obscenely wide leather belts that prompted Eggerton to question whether they would ever slip through the loops in a pair of pants. He found a skinny, red-haired clerk with a terrible acne condition sitting behind the counter, reading a comic book about some sort of snarling muscular military hero named Sgt. Rock. The kid with the pimples wore a T-shirt himself, but it wasn't anything similar to what Eggerton was looking for. The kid's T-shirt said: "Mötley Crüe." The kid was also dressed in fatigue-green military-style cargo pants that were tucked smartly into a pair of high, tightly-laced black boots spit-shined to a hard gloss. Eggerton stood at the counter for three or four minutes before the kid noticed he was there.

Eggerton was mildly amused by the scene. He wondered whether the kid with the pimples was Clyde and quickly concluded that he was not. Clyde, Eggerton was sure, would be paying more attention to the operation of the store: the display of inventory, the receipts in the cash register, future marketing schemes similar to the one that had drawn Eggerton here today. Anyway, when the comic book reader at long last acknowledged his presence, Eggerton asked where he could find the surplus pea-green T-shirts advertised in the newspaper. The kid barely looked up from the exploits of Sgt. Rock, pointed toward a rack near the rear of the story, and said: "Der." And with that, he returned to his comic book.

Eggerton raised his eyebrows, but got the message. He found the T-shirts, selected a half-dozen one size too big (Eggerton was careful to allow for shrinkage in the washing machine), presented the comic book reader with his coupon and made the purchase.

"Beg?" the kid asked.

My Life With Wings

Eggerton assumed the kid with the pimples wanted to know whether he should insert the T-shirts in a bag. Eggerton elucidated, simply and clearly, "Yeah, beg."

He was handed back the six shirts stuffed roughly into a plastic bag that Eggerton recognized as coming from a nearby supermarket. Obviously, Eggerton deduced, Clyde was shaving overhead by re-using begs. A true surplus man to the end, Eggerton concluded, with more than just a grudging sense of admiration for this fellow Clyde.

Eggerton couldn't recall whether Clyde also carried surplus Army cots, but he decided it was worth a try. Of course, he would need somebody to go to the store for him. He couldn't very well walk in there flapping his wings, could he? What would the kid with the pimples say? Wegs? His first thought was to ask Crane to go, but he remembered Crane kept the $7 left over from the groceries and he didn't want to spend more money on the cot than he had to. So he decided to call Woody. Yes, he decided to ask his friend Woody to pick up a cot for him at Clyde's Army-Navy Surplus Store. He called his friend.

Eggerton waited for Woody in the secret attic room. He sat perched on a stool he carried up from the kitchen, looking out through the window at the street below. Whenever he heard a car enter the street, Eggerton would crane his neck to catch a glimpse of the vehicle as it appeared through the foliage of some tall maple trees that lined the yards of his neighbors.

Several times, Eggerton found himself disappointed when he discovered the car didn't belong to Woody. Finally, though, Woody's color-of-an-acid-rain-polluted-ocean Buick Skylark pulled onto the street and found a parking place right in front of Eggerton's home.

Eggerton leaned forward. Does he have the cot? Does he have the cot? Yes! Yes! Woody was struggling to pull a parcel out of the back seat—it was large, paper-wrapped and tied together with rough twine. Obviously, the kid with the pimples or perhaps even the proprietor, that savvy entrepreneur Clyde himself, folded and wrapped the cot in dark brown wrapping paper and heavy twine so Woody would be able to tote it home in a neat and convenient bundle. Clearly, when the kid said "Beg?" to Woody, Woody answered "Yes, a beg would do quite nicely, thank you."

Eggerton flew down the stairs, arriving at the front door just as Woody approached the narrow flagstone walk in the front of the house. He peered out the door at his friend: Woody was perspiring heavily under the weight of the cot, the rolls of his fat belly bouncing as he trudged along. He wore a white T-shirt with a V-neck, a style Woody favored, even in winter when he wore white V-neck shirts under his white dress shirts at the Happy Buffalo Wing. (Woody, Eggerton knew, was habitually parsimonious when it came to clothes; it was painfully obvious that his white dress shirts were fashioned of the cheapest fabrics because the V-neck of his T-shirt was negligibly yet always plainly visible beneath his dress shirt.)

In addition to the V-neck T-shirt, Woody wore a pair of plaid shorts cut much too high for his girth. His two fleshy thighs, which poured out of his shorts, quaked as he walked up the flagstone path. What's more, Woody's T-shirt separated itself from his short pants, which meant his hairy belly was visible, hanging over the waist of the shorts, making Woody look ever fatter. Eggerton wished he could open the door and step onto the flagstone walk so he could help his friend with the weight of the bundle, but he stayed indoors knowing that if a neighbor saw him, the secret of his wings would be out.

Finally, Woody arrived at the front door and just as he was about to knock Eggerton threw the door open and invited Woody inside, quickly. Woody entered the home.

"You're in luck," Woody said. "They had one left. The kid in the store said they never have a problem selling these babies. I guess people need cots."

Woody took out a handkerchief and wiped the sweat off his forehead. His face was red.

"I think it's a good price—$29.95," he said. "Pay me when you have a chance. Got something to drink? A beer? Maybe an iced tea? Where do you want this baby?"

Woody dug a pack of cigarettes out of a pocket in his shorts. He lit one with a cheap butane lighter, flicking on the flame with a snap of his meaty thumb. He drew heavily on the tobacco.

Eggerton said he had some bottled beer and Woody said that would be fine. Eggerton retrieved a beer for his friend. Woody's eyes lit up when he saw the dark brown bottle. He twisted the cap off, leaned his head back and swallowed hard. Refreshed, he smiled and wiped his lips with a sleeve, then took another drag from his cigarette and allowed the smoke to escape lazily from his mouth and nose.

"I love beer," he said. "Beer, butts and baseball. That's what makes America great."

Woody drew hard again on his cigarette, and then swallowed some more beer. Eggerton watched his friend's Adam's Apple bounce as the beer washed down his throat.

After taking his second drink from the bottle, Woody wiped his mouth on his sleeve again. And then, he regarded Eggerton. A look of deep perplexity crossed his face.

Woody was never one to ignore the obvious.

Finally, he said, "What's with the wings?"

Eggerton told him what happened, albeit in an abbreviated version of the story. He also told Woody that Crane was looking into the prospects of amputation.

"Oh! Christ! No! You don't want to do that!"

Eggerton asked why not.

"You want to keep those babies. I bet you can parlay those babies into big bucks. I bet a lot of people would be interested in your story. You can be like that guy with the big nose."

"The big nose?"

"Yeah, the Elephant Man. Didn't he get rich because he was born with a really big nose? Isn't that the story with him?"

Eggerton told Woody the Elephant Man didn't have a really big nose.

Woody took another long drink from his beer. He wiped his lips again across his sleeve. "Wasn't his mother scared by an elephant? Is that why they called him the Elephant Man?"

Woody wanted to know whether Eggerton's mother was scared by a bird.

"Falcons can be kinda scary," Woody said.

Eggerton said he didn't think the story of the Elephant Man had anything to do with somebody's mother being scared by an elephant. He didn't feel it necessary to answer the question regarding his mother and a bird.

Woody pondered that thought, swallowed some more beer and drew again on his cigarette. "Still," Woody said, "you don't want to lose those babies. There can be big bucks in this for you. Maybe a Netflix movie. Or the tabloids would pay for an interview. Hell, if the Elephant Man could get a Netflix movie, you could get one of those babies, too."

"Don't be silly," Eggerton said. "I don't want to be a sideshow freak."

"Suit yourself," Woody said.

He drained the remainder of his beer and put the empty on the floor. He asked Eggerton where he wanted the cot. Eggerton told him the attic would be fine.

"You bought a cot so you could put it in the attic?"

Eggerton shrugged his feathers.

Woody carried the cot up two flights of stairs with Eggerton helping, albeit slightly, because he still had trouble controlling his wings and they flounced around during the trip up the stairs. From time to time, as the two men ascended the stairs with the cot, Eggerton caught Woody staring at him. Woody quickly averted his eyes, but Eggerton needed no more convincing that he should stay indoors as much as possible until he resolved what to do about his wings.

If his friend Woody couldn't control his stares, Eggerton could imagine how total strangers would react.

Finally, Woody and Eggerton made it to the attic and found the entranceway for the secret room. Woody was just barely able to squeeze through the opening and, once inside the secret attic room, he perspired heavily while taking long, painful gasps of air.

Indeed, he looked in no shape to continue manual labor. So, Eggerton dragged the cot through on his own. It was easy enough to set up.

Within a few seconds, the cot was unfolded and sitting alongside the stool in the stark little room.

Eggerton felt himself growing weary and remarked to himself that the cot looked inviting, but he remembered his guest so he suggested they return to the kitchen, promising Woody a fresh beer.

"Good idea," said Woody. "I could use another one of those babies."

Woody and Eggerton made their way out of the secret attic room. Eggerton led Woody back to the kitchen, where he gave him a fresh bottle of beer. Woody used the bottom of his T-shirt to wipe the sweat

My Life With Wings

from his face, exposing his rather hairy belly which, Eggerton couldn't help but notice, was dotted with ringworm. Woody lit another cigarette, drank from the new bottle, glanced at his watch and said he had to run home to prepare for work.

"Keep those babies," Woody said, gesturing toward Eggerton's wings, as he exited the house.

Eggerton watched as his friend walked down the flagstone path. Suddenly, Woody raised and lowered his arms, as though he were flapping a pair of his own wings. As he flapped his arms, ash fell off the cigarette he held between two chubby fingers in his right hand, and beer splashed out of the bottle he held in his left hand. Woody flapped his arms three times, and each time he did it he lost ash from his cigarette and beer from his bottle.

Chapter Eight

Eggerton flopped down on the cot, belly first. He was right: the cot was as soft as a bed of downy feathers; indeed, he fell asleep quite quickly. He had a very unusual dream. It was unusual for a number of reasons. First, Eggerton didn't think he dreamed a lot, and it was rare that, when he did dream, he remembered many of the details.

This time, though, the dream remained quite vivid in his memory, long after he woke up. In fact, the details of the dream weighed so heavily on his mind that he found it good therapy to write a description of the dream. He would have liked to have sat at his Cinzano table on the terra cotta patio listening to Bird Parker songs while he wrote out the details of his dream, but he wasn't able to do that for obvious reasons. Instead, he decided to sit on the hard wooden floor in the secret attic room, wings spread behind him, to write out the details of his dream.

First, though, he would need paper. And a pencil. He left the secret attic room and wandered around the house, in search of suitable materials to tell his story.

He kept an old coffee can filled with pens and pencils on a counter in the kitchen, so that's where he headed first. He spent several minutes rooting through the can.

He came across several Bic pens—the old-fashioned type with the clear barrels, each showing dwindling supplies of ink. He knew they would never do. He found several other pens: old ballpoints that he hadn't used for years, certain they would skip or form little blue blotches as he dragged them across the page. He eschewed them as well. Finally, he found a common pencil, a No. 2 medium Dixon Tinconderoga with a sharp point and an eraser virtually intact, and seemed satisfied.

Next, he searched for paper. Amazingly, he found no ready supply—no unused steno pad, no shrink-wrapped ream of computer printer paper, no sheaf of rough-hewn typing paper left over from the days when people actually typed on typewriters. But he did find a scrap of paper here and a scrap of paper there. Here, in fact, is the inventory of paper Eggerton accumulated as he searched the house:

One sheet of 8.5-by-11 inch paper, goldenrod in color, that had been folded and left under the wiper blade of his car windshield. The front of the paper announced the opening of a local pizza emporium and promised a $1 discount if the bearer of the goldenrod circular purchased a pizza before April 30, a date which had long since passed. Nevertheless, the rear of the paper was blank and Eggerton knew it would suit his purposes.

A 9-by-12 inch envelope, white in color, that had contained a catalogue of fly fishing supplies. Eggerton recalled receiving the catalogue in the mail several days ago. He had, indeed, been puzzled by the envelope—the upper left corner simply contained a post office box. After opening the envelope, using his finger to roughly rip through the top vertical seam, he discovered the catalogue and was disappointed because he had no interest in fly fishing. So he quickly tossed away the catalogue as well as the envelope, but—happy day!—he neglected to take out the trash last week so the envelope remained available to him in what had clearly turned out to be a time of need. Sometimes, he concluded, you find yourself lucky.

My Life With Wings

The back of his last paycheck stub. The stub measured 4-by-8.5 inches. The front of the stub contained various pieces of data regarding his salary—gross wages, net wages, overtime payments, taxes withheld, and so on, printed in a computer-generated, sans serif typeface selected, Eggerton supposed, more for its utilitarianism than for its aesthetic value. Eggerton never kept his stubs, which he knew was probably foolish, but for some reason he kept this one and now he had his third piece of paper.

A completely clean (on both sides!) sheet of copy machine paper. It was in perfect condition: no folds, no scribblings, no erasures. Eggerton thought very carefully, and failed to recall how the paper found its way into his house. But one does not ask questions at times like this, one simply counts one's lucky stars, eh? It was a valuable piece for the collection, because both sides would be available for use.

The cash register receipt from Clyde's Army-Navy Surplus Store for the T-shirts he purchased some weeks past. It was small, no more than 2 inches by 4 inches, but it would do in a pinch.

Eggerton now had five sheets of paper—the goldenrod pizza advertisement, the white fly fishing catalogue envelope, the clean piece of copy paper, the paycheck stub and the cash register receipt from Clyde's. Actually, he had six pieces—on the way back to the secret attic room, he stopped off in the bathroom and retrieved the flowery pink bas relief napkin on which he had recorded the time (to the minute) when he discovered his wings. And, perhaps, Eggerton could even argue he had seven pieces, because during his search for paper he came across one of those manila file folders common to most offices and he was certain he could write on the manila file folder, if push came to shove. In the meantime, he deposited his six pieces of paper into the manila file envelope and retreated to the secret attic room where he intended to record the details of his dream and do whatever other serious writing he would find necessary.

Across the front of the manila folder, Eggerton wrote: *My Life With Wings.*

49

Chapter Nine

To Eggerton's best recollection, his dream lasted the entire time he was asleep. Thinking back on his dream, Eggerton concluded it started the instant he fell asleep—which was within seconds after he flopped down on the cot—and ended the instant he opened his eyes, which Eggerton calculated to be 14 hours after he went to sleep. (Eggerton was quite weary, having not slept at all in the two days since he first grew wings.)

A 14-hour dream was most unusual, but could anybody suggest Eggerton's life hadn't taken a few unusual turns lately? Eggerton wondered whether anyone else dreams for 14 hours. Anyway, here is Eggerton's dream, written out in longhand on the back of the goldenrod pizza advertisement, exactly as it happened, according to Eggerton:

It is December 14, 1903. I am standing on a sandy dune in, I think, North Carolina. It is very cold and windy. I have a brother in my dream. In real life, I don't have a brother but in this dream

I have an older brother. We flip a coin. I call heads. I win. Shit. My brother extends his hand. We shake. I don't have wings in the dream, for which I'm grateful. I figure if I have to be a freak while I'm awake, I should not have to be a freak when I'm asleep. Behind me is an airplane. It has a wingspan of 40 feet, 4 inches, and a length of 24 feet. The wings are made of fabric stretched over slats of ash.

This is all my brother's idea. I figure if he is so sure it will work, he should do the dicey stuff. He laughs and tells me I'm such a kidder. I climb aboard and sit at the controls. I want to do this like I want to piss in the face of a Spanish fighting bull.

I'm not the adventurous type. I like to go to bars and pick up women, although since it is 1903 you wouldn't expect to find many women hanging around bars. But, hey. This is my dream. In my dream, women hang around bars even if it is 1903 and they always seem to buy my bullshit and go home with me.

Anyway, my brother starts the engine. It is very loud, almost deafening. I hear a muffled "give-em-hell" yell from my brother.

Yeah, I think, screw you, give 'em hell yourself. I need a drink.

Suddenly, the plane starts moving. I glance over at my brother. He is smiling broadly. He gives me the thumbs up sign. I give him the F-You sign.

He starts laughing. You are such a kidder, he yells.

I turn back around and face forward. I push ahead on the throttle and the plane begins moving faster, taxiing across the hard sandy surface. I have never flown an airplane in my life but my brother, who thinks he's oh-so-smart, says don't worry, it will work.

Yeah, I say, if you're so goddamned sure of yourself, why don't you fly the goddamned thing.

Ha ha, he says, I'm such a kidder.

The beast is picking up speed. I hunker down and brace myself against the wind, which is quite chilly. Damn, I think my ears are frostbitten. Why the fuck did I agree to this nonsense?

My Life With Wings

Now, the engine is so loud I'm sure it is going to explode. The plane is really moving. The cold wind whips past my face, giving me windburn, I am sure. Suddenly, the plane is airborne. By just a foot or two. Not too high, but the plane has definitely left the ground. But just for a second.

I feel, well, I feel a sense of exhiliration. Yes, exhiliration. Suddenly, I have stopped noticing the icy winds splashing me in the face. Instead, I feel a burning sensation in my chest. My sense of excitement keeps growing. I smile broadly, even start laughing.

Gosh, this feels good.

Maybe my brother is a genius. Maybe the jerk does know what he's talking about.

I wonder whether I have had this all wrong from the beginning. I waste my time, hanging around bars, looking for easy sex from women. My brother, on the other hand, is always looking ahead. Thinking up screwy ideas that, in the final analysis, make a lot of sense. Like building a machine that can actually fly like a bird.

Maybe he is a genius, after all.

Maybe...

Maybe...

Maybe...shit.

The plane touches down again. Hard. The undercarriage shatters and a wheel flies off. The plane skids across the dunes. The damage is heavy, but the plane manages to stay intact. As for me, that's another matter. I throw up. Of course, the plane is moving forward when that happens so the vomit splashes back into my face. My goggles are caked in it. Shit, I hate when that happens.

I also notice that I have pissed in my pants.

The plane is spinning now as it skids to a stop. I'm dizzy, a wreck. I can do nothing but hold on and hope it doesn't flip over. If the plane flips over, I could be crushed.

Suddenly, I notice the engine is still running. I kill the engine with my vomitty fingers and the plane skids to a stop. I think I have a nosebleed as well. Maybe I bumped my head. Maybe a concussion. Wouldn't that be fan-fucking-tastic?

My heart is pounding very hard. I am very excited but happy to be alive. My brother runs up to me. He is out of breath. He asks if I'm OK and I say what do you think, asshole, I threw up and pissed in my pants? I also wonder whether I shit myself.

He laughs, tells me I'm a kidder. I want to punch him. A newspaper photographer is on the dunes, and he snaps a picture. Tomorrow, there will be a picture of me in the newspaper with vomit on my goggles and piss stains on my pants. Later, my brother tells me the plane was aloft for no more than a second, and that its altitude was maybe a foot. No more than that. No matter, he says, we achieved flight.

We? I ask. What's this we shit?

He laughs again. He tells me he thinks he knows how to fix the plane so it doesn't crash after only a second or two in the air. He says this is a very exciting time, to be on the verge of flying high with the birds. He looks skyward and tells me he thinks it will be possible to one day fly to the moon.

The moon? Really? I think my brother is nuts. All I want to do is go home and take a bath, then go out to a bar and find a woman for sex and companionship. Again, this in 1903 and in 1903 you didn't find many women hanging around bars, but this is my dream and it can end any way I want so if you don't see it my way you can go fuck yourself.

Which is what I tell my brother after he tells me he wants to fix the plane. "Oh yeah?" I say to him, "Why don't you go fuck yourself?"

He laughs and tells me I'm such a kidder.

After Eggerton wrote those words he read them and then read them again. He was a bit surprised at the hostility of the narrative voice, which was his own, but he decided that was the voice that spoke in the dream, and one certainly doesn't argue with one's dreams, does one?

Otherwise, it didn't seem like much of a story—certainly, not one that would last fourteen hours—but that is essentially what happened. After reading over the description of his dream a third time, Eggerton concluded that if he tore up the paper and wrote it over again, he would not tell it any other way. He wasn't sure what he planned to do with the description of his dream.

For now, he took the sheet of paper and put it in the manila file folder with the other sheets of paper, including the pink bas relief napkin on which he recorded the exact date and time he discovered he had grown wings. Next, he put the manila file folder under his cot. He was hungry, so he went to the kitchen, prepared a cold sandwich and ate it in the secret attic room while reading and re-reading the description of his dream.

Later, Martin called and said he talked to Woody, and Woody told him about the wings thing, and could he come over and see for himself? Eggerton wasn't sure he appreciated Woody telling his secret, but he couldn't recall that he, well, told Woody not to tell anyone. He also wasn't sure he appreciated being gawked at, even by his friend Martin. But he was anxious for some company so he told Martin it was OK for him to come over.

Chapter Ten

Martin never went out without a jacket and tie. Often, he wore a suit. His shoes were always shined to a hard gloss, and he was one of the few people Eggerton knew who wore garters to keep his socks up. Eggerton knew Martin wore garters because he occasionally played racquetball with him. When Martin took off his pants in the locker room, Eggerton couldn't help but notice his friend wore garters with tight elastic bands strapped snugly around his calves. The elastic bands left red indentations in Martin's calves. Nobody else in the locker room wore garter belts. Martin was, by the way, a terrible racquetball player; he lost each game they played and seemed to have less than a vague comprehension of the rules. Beating Martin at racquetball provided Eggerton with absolutely no fulfillment.

Anyway, with the exception of their times on the racquetball court, Eggerton could never recall seeing Martin without a jacket, white shirt and tie, and Eggerton found all that very unusual about Martin, inasmuch as Martin didn't have what you would call a real job. He left the copy desk (where he always came to work dressed impeccably) to become a freelance writer and, indeed, had been making something of a living at it now for three years.

As such, he had no boss to impress nor dress code to follow. Nevertheless, every morning, Martin rose, showered, shaved and dressed in a jacket and tie. And he always put on his garters because he always felt as though his socks were sliding down around his ankles, even though there was more than sufficient elastic in the socks themselves to keep them up sans garters. But it was just one of those unexplainable yet nagging feelings Martin endured in life, so he wore garters.

Otherwise, Martin was hardly carving out himself a very prosperous life in the world of freelance writing. He never seemed to lack for jobs, to be sure, but most paid very poorly. He lived in a tiny, pre-furnished studio apartment. He found the mattress on his bed quite uncomfortable—it was far too soft to his liking. But since he could not afford to purchase a bed and mattress of his own he endured the too-soft mattress.

And as for always dressing in a white shirt, tie and jacket—and often a suit—well, in truth, he only owned three white shirts, three ties, two sports jackets, two pairs of slacks, and one suit (grey, pinstriped.) His underwear and sock drawers were also rather lean. Martin often washed his clothes (the apartment did have a washer and dryer) every other day. He found, though, that he was able to get away with using just half the detergent recommended by the label on the bottle of detergent.)

Eggerton dozed off on the cot, but awakened quite suddenly when he heard a series of sharp raps on the front door of the house. He rose from the cot and swung open the window of the secret attic room. Below, he saw the top of Martin's balding head. Martin was vigorously striking the front door.

"Martin! Stop that!" Eggerton shouted.

Martin looked up and waved. Eggerton saw his friend wore a gray pinstripe suit, white shirt and red tie. There were little horseshoes embroidered into the red tie. Eggerton couldn't help but notice a tiny gravy stain on the tie, just below the 14th horseshoe (from the bottom) and wondered whether Martin noticed the stain, inasmuch as Martin was fastidious to the core. Martin, Eggerton concluded, must have dressed in a hurry. Eggerton made his way downstairs from the secret attic room.

At first, Martin said nothing as Eggerton opened the front door for him. The two men stood in the foyer, neither talking. Martin simply stared at Eggerton, and then slowly started walking circles around him as he gazed at his wings.

Finally, Martin said, "Fuckin' amazing. Woody was fuckin' right, man. You've got fuckin' wings."

Eggerton shrugged. He felt uncomfortable. Why did Martin have to stare?

"Knock it off," Eggerton said.

Martin refused to stop staring.

"Fuckin' amazing," he said.

"Do you want a beer?" Eggerton asked. He thought Martin might stop staring if he gave him a beer. After all, it had worked with Woody.

"No," Martin said.

"Well, quit staring," Eggerton said. "I'm not the main attraction in a freak show."

Martin said he was sorry, but you had to admit a guy with wings was fuckin' amazing.

"Let's talk," Martin said.

Eggerton said he'd prefer to talk upstairs, so he led Martin to the secret attic room. Eggerton sat down on the cot, letting his wings go limp. There was no place for Martin to sit except on the floor. Martin decided to stand. He didn't want to wrinkle his trousers.

Eggerton told Martin the story of how he woke up one morning with wings. He told him that Crane—whom Martin knew casually—was investigating the amputation option. He told him he hadn't been to work since his wings first appeared, but he wasn't sure how long the newspaper management would buy the story of his prolonged illness. After all, he had been telling them he couldn't shake a nasty head cold.

He wondered whether he should show Martin his fake sneeze and fake cough. Although he had called the newspaper back daily reporting that he couldn't shake his cold, no one at the paper had yet questioned his truthfulness. Lately, though, he wondered whether somebody at the newspaper would show signs of skepticism about his lingering illness, and at that point he would have to offer the fake cough and sneeze. He continued to fret over whether his act would be believable and thought it might be a good idea to try out his fake cough and fake sneeze on

Martin who could perhaps offer an opinion on whether the act was truly believable. But he quickly dismissed the idea, doubting whether Martin would really give him a truthful opinion. Instead, he suspected Martin would simply say, "Yeah, it sounds real."

He also thought about telling Martin that he preferred to sleep on the cot, and how he had a 14-hour dream about crashing in a primitive airplane, but he decided Martin didn't need to know that information, either.

But he did tell Martin that Woody thought he should sell his story to a TV or movie producer, and he regarded Woody's idea as a joke.

"Oh, Woody is on the right track," Martin said, "but don't sell your story to the movies or TV, at least not yet."

Martin told Eggerton he would write a book about Eggerton's life with wings. He started outlining the book for Eggerton: Chapter One would be a sort of "hook" chapter—what life is like with wings—working, playing, dating. Chapter Two would be Eggerton's early years: childhood, education, professional life, marriage, divorce.

"Divorce?" Eggerton asked. "Do we have to get into that?"

Martin frowned. He told Eggerton he had to be totally honest about himself.

He continued. Chapter Three would center on the morning it happened: the morning he awoke with wings. Martin said this chapter should be particularly dramatic.

"You really want to grab the reader by the gut," Martin said.

Chapter Four would follow Eggerton to work. He would talk about a typical day as a newspaper copy editor with wings. Chapters Five, Six and Seven would be about other aspects of life with wings…cooking, cleaning, using the toilet, that sort of thing. Martin wondered whether they could write a whole chapter just on what type of clothes a man with wings would be apt to wear.

Eggerton regarded himself. He was still wearing the black and white striped boxer shorts he had on when he woke up three days ago with wings. He still hadn't bathed, remembering that he promised himself a sponge bath. He was sure he developed a rather pungent odor by now, and that Crane, Woody and Martin were too polite to mention it. Absently, he felt his cheek and chin—a hard stubble; Eggerton needed a shave.

My Life With Wings

He definitely promised himself that once Martin left, he would head for the bathroom and sponge off and then have himself a good shave.

Suddenly, he realized Martin had been talking while he was pondering matters of personal hygiene.

"Of course, I think Chapter Eight will be the best chapter of all," Martin said.

"Huh?"

"Chapter Eight," Martin said. "Surely you agree with me about Chapter Eight."

Eggerton said he was sorry, he was daydreaming and missed the whole discussion about Chapter Eight.

Martin didn't seem to mind.

"Sex," Martin said. "Every story needs sex. We'll do a whole chapter on sex with wings."

"Don't be silly," Eggerton said.

Martin said he wasn't being silly. He wanted to know whether Eggerton was seeing anybody at the moment. No, Eggerton said, he hadn't had a date since Mouse walked out on him.

"Any chance of getting together again with Mouse?"

"I should say not!"

"Don't dismiss the idea too quickly. Call her and say you have wings and a book deal, and that you need to do a chapter on sex. I bet she'll give you a good humping again just for the sake of literature."

Eggerton heard enough. He told Martin he didn't want to talk about the book anymore. Martin seemed surprised. He told Eggerton there could be a lucrative book deal in this for the both of them. He proposed a 50-50 split on the book; as far as other property rights were concerned—movies, TV, computer games and so on—that would be open to negotiation, but he could see Eggerton taking home 75 percent of the pie. Martin said as far as he was concerned, his job would be finished after the book is written and sold.

"Maybe I'd want a hand in the screenplay," he added, "but we can talk about that."

Eggerton told Martin he'd think it over. He rose from the cot and left the secret attic room. Martin followed. On the way down the stairs, Eggerton asked Martin about his book on Bashful Bladder Syndrome.

Martin said the book was proceeding along nicely—that he had interviewed a handful of men who admitted to being unable to pee in public lavatories, briefly telling Eggerton about the prize of the bunch, a shilly-shallying micturator named Griffin who was intelligent, articulate, educated and willing to go on the record with his story, kind of sort of.

Soon, Martin said, he would expect to wrap up the testimonial part of the book and concentrate on the medical aspects of the affliction. Nevertheless, Martin said, he'd be prepared to put the Bashful Bladder Syndrome book aside and throw himself fully into the book about Eggerton and his life with wings.

"Can I call you, maybe tomorrow, and we can talk more about this?" Martin asked. "I'd like to work up an outline; you know, have something to show my literary agent."

Eggerton said he wasn't sure where he'd be tomorrow. Actually, Eggerton had a pretty good idea. He was sure he would still be in the house, probably in the secret attic room, still thinking things out about the damned wings. Unless, of course, he woke up tomorrow and didn't have wings. If that happened, he'd probably be at his desk at the newspaper because he didn't think he could afford to miss more work. Clearly, he believed, the people at the newspaper were growing suspicious of his extended absence. Nevertheless, Eggerton was quite certain he'd be home tomorrow, but he decided Martin didn't need to know that because he knew he wouldn't be in the mood to field a call from Martin to talk over the literary as well as entrepreneurial possibilities of a life with wings. So he told Martin not to call, he might be out.

"Then the next day?"

Eggerton shrugged. He knew that if he put Martin off again, Martin would conclude he didn't want to do the book, and then Martin would probably question the value of their friendship. Eggerton did, after all, want to stay friends with Martin.

"Sure," he said. "Call then."

Martin promised he would. Then, he told Eggerton he thought his wings were fuckin' amazing. He left Eggerton's house and walked out to the street over the flagstone path. Eggerton watched him leave. He noticed there was a certain bounce to Martin's step; obviously, Mar-

My Life With Wings

tin was quite happy with himself. Eggerton couldn't understand why. "Certainly," Eggerton thought, "if I did decide to write a book about my life with wings, I wouldn't need Martin to write it for me. I'd write it myself. I am, after all, a newspaper copy editor." While he was mulling over that thought and watching Martin leave by the flagstone path, he saw Martin raise and lower his arms—in that flapping wing motion, exactly as Woody had done so the day before.

Odd, Eggerton thought. But then, Eggerton couldn't deny that most occurrences in his life seemed odd these days.

Chapter Eleven

After Martin left, Eggerton spent an uneventful day at home. He sat in the kitchen listening to the radio for a bit, then grew bored and restless. So, he went up to the secret attic room where he stood in front of the open window, arms folded in front of him, wings folded behind him, gazing down at the street below.

Occasionally, somebody would walk along the sidewalk, and Eggerton regarded them as they strolled by his house. He saw Mrs. Hedron, a short but robust roly-poly woman with a waddle like a duck, who lived two doors down in a neat, two-story Tudor home that had been freshly repainted a year ago in a shade of eggshell white. She came lumbering down the block, toting a two-wheeled shopping cart laden with groceries. Eggerton discovered he could see clearly into Mrs. Hedron's bag of groceries from above because his eyesight had grown particularly keen. He could tell Mrs. Hedron was fond of Saltine crackers (crispy variety), diet root beer (store brand) and tangelos. After Mrs. Hedron walked by and disappeared beneath an elm tree out of Eggerton's view, no one else came down the block for 30 minutes or more.

But Eggerton's patience was rewarded when Dr. Hitchcock drove up and parked his shiny black vintage Pontiac Firebird on the street. Dr. Hitchcock was 73 and still practicing medicine. Eggerton thought a Pontiac Firebird was a bit sporty for someone of Dr. Hitchcock's age; nevertheless, Eggerton would be the last person to deny Dr. Hitchcock the right to drive a sporty car. Dr. Hitchcock lived next-door, his home separated Eggerton's house from Mrs. Hedron's house. Eggerton thought Dr. Hitchcock could be cranky at times; whenever he saw Dr. Hitchcock on the block Eggerton would give his neighbor an enthusiastic greeting—"Hullo Doc!" was a typical salutation—but Dr. Hitchcock rarely had much more to say to Eggerton than, "Morning" or, if it were late, "Evening" or, if it were mid-day, "Afternoon."

From his perch high above the street, Eggerton could tell Dr. Hitchcock was losing a lot of hair on his head, and a quick count indicated the physician possesed less than a thousand hairs. Eggerton made a mental note to count the hairs on Dr. Hitchcock's head the next time he peered down at him from above.

After parking his car, Dr. Hitchcock hurried into his home, refusing Eggerton's unspoken plea that he dawdle at the curb so that he may have a few more seconds to study the creases in his forehead or the waxy gray hair growing from his ears or, even, the dots of perspiration gathering just above his collar.

The only other person Eggerton saw that afternoon was Crowe, a landscaper who mowed Dr. Hitchcock's lawn. Oh, but Crowe presented a feast for Eggerton's nictating membrane! A beefy, shirtless and sunburned man of about 50 who smokes unfiltered Camel cigarettes, Eggerton watched closely as Crowe wrestled with a noisy lawnmower in uneven horizontal paths across Dr. Hitchcock's front yard. The leafy canopy of a large maple tree blocked off part of Dr. Hitchcock's lawn from Eggerton's view, so Eggerton could only see Crowe for a few seconds each time the sweaty laborer made a pass with the lawnmower. Nevertheless, good old Crowe did provide Eggerton with a visible feast for nearly twenty minutes and he was grateful for the diversion.

From above, Eggerton could see Crowe's generally hairless chest, although a few sweaty black hairs grew out of his nipples. Specifically, Eggerton counted 17 hairs growing from the right nipple and 11 growing from the left. Crowe also has touches of psoriasis on his elbows and seborrhea on his palms. His right forefinger is heavily callused and Eggerton couldn't help but notice a pustule on Crowe's left shoulder blade. Crowe needed a shave, no question about that. His ears were dirty as well.

Once, when Crowe made a pass with the mower walking toward Eggerton's house, Eggerton noticed a wayward blade of grass found its way into Crowe's left nostril and was poking out ever so slightly. A few passes later, Eggerton saw the blade of grass was no longer there, and he wondered whether Crowe—under cover of the maple tree—had either unknowingly inhaled the blade of grass and was now metabolizing it in his cardiopulmonary system or, more likely, simply sneezed it out. Strangely, though, Eggerton noticed no traces of snot on Crowe's upper lip. Eggerton exhaled and sighed. Obviously, the mystery of what happened to the blade of grass imbedded in Crowe's nose would forever remain a mystery to everyone but Crowe, of course. Certainly, Eggerton couldn't see himself descending to the street level, wings akimbo, with the intent of confronting Crowe as to the fate of a single blade of grass. No sir. That would never do.

The remainder of Crowe's performance on Dr. Hitchcock's front lawn turned out to be rather uneventful. Eggerton noticed a mole on the back of Crowe's neck and a tattoo on his arm. The tattoo had faded over the years and was barely discernable, even to Eggerton's keen vision, but after studying it for several mower passes Eggerton deduced the tattoo had been inscribed during Crowe's service in the Navy, and that it included a tattoo artist's conception of an aircraft carrier as well as the legend "Death from Above" lettered underneath the carrier in neat black and blue sans-serif printing.

Death from above? Whatever could that mean?

Finally, Crowe completed the front yard. He pushed the mower up a ramp onto the bed of a truck, entered the truck cab and drove off. As Crowe's truck left the street, Eggerton saw some paint had chipped off the corner of the truck's license plate. Just a nick, Eggerton observed. Off the upper right hand corner. No more than a sliver. Hardly noticeable.

Chapter Twelve

Eggerton waited at the window for somebody else to walk by, but no one did for the longest time. Soon, Eggerton found himself growing weary. So, he retreated from the window, let himself fall face-first onto the cot, and fell asleep.

He awoke as he felt his body nudged. He also heard what he thought was his name, only he could just make out the first syllable each time it was enunciated.

"Egg. . . .

"Egg. . .

"Egg. . ."

He heard.

He opened his eyes. It was Crane.

"The door was open so I let myself in," Crane said. "I have news for you."

Eggerton sat up on the cot and allowed his eyes to focus. Crane was standing before him, dressed in white, as usual.

"Hello," said Eggerton.

"Hello," said Crane.

Suddenly, Eggerton noticed Crane was not alone. Standing just by the door of the secret attic room was a large, burly fellow with a shaved head and barrel chest. He wore baggy gym shorts decorated with vertical stripes and a gray sleeveless undershirt with the message "Property of Hawks Athletic Department" stenciled neatly across the front in Roman block letters. His arms were well-muscled, as were his legs. His neck was thick. He smelled of talc. Eggerton noticed that an icepack was bandaged to the young man's right ankle.

Crane realized he should introduce his new friend to Eggerton. "That's Hendrix," Crane said. "He plays linebacker for his college team."

Eggerton regarded the fellow closely while silence hung over the secret attic room. Finally, Eggerton said, "Go Hawks." Hendrix stared at Eggerton and shrugged. "Thanks," he said.

Crane met Hendrix that morning. Hendrix was injured at practice, twisting an ankle while making a tackle. Hendrix told the coach it was no big deal but the trainer feared a broken bone and insisted Hendrix go to the hospital for an x-ray.

Hendrix reluctantly complied and, as it turned out, the x-ray was negative, showing only a sprain. Crane was called in to counsel Hendrix on how to rehab the ankle after it healed.

During their brief encounter Hendix mentioned to Crane that he, too, was a physical therapy major in college because he knew he would need a career to fall back on in the event he did not make it to the pros. When Crane asked him why he selected physical therapy as a major, Hendrix replied with a shrug, "I like the white uniforms." The two became instant friends.

Hendrix stepped forward and examined Eggerton with wide, bloodshot eyes.

"Fuck me runnin'," said Hendrix.

Crane shot Hendrix an icy glance. Hendrix quickly shut his mouth and retreated into the shadows of the secret attic room.

Eggerton was still groggy, but anxious to hear what Crane had to say. "News?" he asked. "You said you have news?"

Crane nodded.

My Life With Wings

"I tried to call several times today, but you didn't answer," Crane said.

Eggerton could understand that. Indeed, he had become a sound sleeper in recent days. And since there was no phone in the secret attic room, it is entirely likely Crane called and Eggerton hadn't heard the phone. As for his cellphone, well, Eggerton wasn't sure where it was. He hadn't seen it in days. He doubted it was even on.

"I'm afraid what I have to tell you won't come as good news," Crane said. He told Eggerton he asked a number of doctors about the surgical removal of wings, and none of them seemed to take the matter seriously. One doctor suggested Eggerton seek a veterinarian.

"I see," said Eggerton. He supposed, deep down, that he expected that sort of response. He couldn't say he was surprised.

Crane kneeled by the cot. He had no qualms about doing so; he was far more supple than Woody and, therefore, able to kneel, but before he did so, he produced a bleached and pressed white handkerchief with a tiny yet to Eggerton highly perceptible fleur-de-lis sewn into the corner, unfolded it, and carefully spread it on the floor, right where he intended to plant his white fabric-sheathed knee.

"Well?" Crane asked.

Eggerton cocked his head and raised his eyebrows.

"Well...what?" Eggerton asked.

"What about the veterinarian?" asked Crane. "Do you think it's worth a try?"

Eggerton said nothing. Was he really serious? Did Crane expect Eggerton to actually go to the office of a veterinarian and sit in the waiting room with the schnauzers with worms and the Labs with ear mites and the Maine coons waiting to be neutered, and then when his name was called to hop up on a Formica countertop and allow a horse doctor to probe his anus with a long cold steel probe?

Huh? Did he really expect all that?

In truth, Crane did expect that. Crane was still not ready to cede his place as the medical expert in Eggerton's little wing-thing problem. He was a physical therapist, dammit—a three-time Sternie winner, dammit—and he aimed to bring some semblance of sense and science to Eggerton's dilemma.

So, Crane said, "Well? What about the veterinarian?"

At which point Eggerton said, "Let me think about it."

Crane seemed satisfied with Eggerton's answer.

"Should The Cranester ask around? You know, check out some vets? See if any of them specialize in. . ."

Eggerton glanced at Crane, waiting with no small amount of dread and trepidation for The Cranester to finish his sentence.

Which he did.

". . . in birds?"

Eggerton blanched.

"I guess it couldn't hurt," he said.

"Good," said The Cranester.

Eggerton heard the snap of a match lighting, then smelled the pungent odor of burnt sulfur. It was Hendrix; he lit a joint. Eggerton and Crane both turned their heads in time to see Hendrix draw hard on the marijuana. Hendrix withdrew the marijuana from his mouth and let the smoke escape slowly from his nose. It formed tight little curlicues as it made its way up to the arched ceiling. Hendrix looked up and noticed Crane and Eggerton were watching him. Silently, he held the joint out to Crane, who waved it off, and then to Eggerton, who waved it off as well. Hendrix shrugged, and took another hit. He rolled his eyes back and coughed.

"I'm soooooo high," he said. "I could soar like a bird."

Suddenly, Hendrix realized that, under the current circumstances, his words could be taken literally. "Soar like a bird!" he laughed. "Get it? Get it? Soar like a bird!"

The linebacker laughed vigorously, then took another hit on the joint.

Crane and Eggerton tried hard to ignore him.

Crane stood, arching his back. He performed some neck rolls. As a physical therapist, Crane always tried to stay loose. He often admonished people to keep their joints loose. "Stay liquid," Crane would say.

"I think you should get out," he told Eggerton.

"What do you mean?"

"Get out. Go places. I bet you haven't been out of the house in several days. Don't take this the wrong way, but you could use a bath."

"I know," said Eggerton, who certainly did not take it the wrong way.

"Listen, pal. Why don't you go clean yourself up, get yourself dressed and let Ol' Cranie treat you to dinner. Then, we could hit some bars I know."

Eggerton blanched. "Don't be silly," he said. "What about. . ."

"What about, 'What?'"

"These," Eggerton said, pointing with both thumbs over both shoulders.

"What about them?"

"I can't go out looking like this."

"Ahh," he said, "the people you'd find in the bars I go to won't even give you a second look. I hang with a physical therapy crowd and, trust me, we've seen everything. The other day I had a beer with another physical therapist I know, his name is Bustard, and he told me he worked with an amputee. The guy was born with six toes and had one removed. So don't worry about my bunch, we've seen it all."

He arched his eyebrows in the direction of Hendrix, who was sitting cross-legged on the floor, toking hard on his marijuana, completely oblivious to the conversation. True, after Hendrix's initial reaction to Eggerton's wingedness, the well-muscled yet decidedly dim linebacker had become preoccupied with smoking his cannabis and little else.

"He wants to be a physical therapist," Crane told Hendrix. "I think he needs to study harder and take the profession with a far deeper sense of commitment, but I think he will be OK. He has a good heart."

Eggerton thought Hendrix was little more than an over-muscled meathead, but he was far more concerned with other matters than Hendrix's future in the profession of physical therapy.

Instead, Eggerton gave some thought to Crane's suggestion of an evening away from home. It would be good to get out, no question about that. He would enjoy a meal in a restaurant. Nothing fancy, a diner would do. They could sit on stools at the counter so he could let his wings dangle behind him.

And after dinner, it would be fun to visit some bars. Eggerton hadn't tasted hard liquor since he woke up with wings.

He knew Crane was right: physical therapists are very willing to overlook physical as well as emotional handicaps. Indeed, outsiders would be welcome in their circle. Just the thought of the night unfolding in front of Eggerton was enough to excite him and make him feel good about himself. Lord, how he really did want to get out, to enjoy an evening away from the dingy secret attic room.

But then he was hit with a cold dose of reality. Goodness, he thought, I have wings. That's a little different than six toes.

So, he told Crane no, he wasn't interested.

"Are you sure?" Crane asked.

"Yes, I am sure," Eggerton said.

Crane shrugged. He glanced at his watch. He didn't really care about the time, but he needed an excuse to leave. Once again, Crane decided, Eggerton was boring him. "Oh, look at the time," he said. "Gotta go. Hey, football star, let's saddle up."

Hendrix leaned over and stubbed out the joint on the floor of the secret attic room. He held onto the roach, cupping it in his palm. He giggled, then wiped his nose with a bare arm.

"I'm sooooo high," he said. "I could flyyyyyyyyyy."

Eggerton started to rise from the cot. Crane waved him off. He told Eggerton he would find his way out of the house.

Eggerton settled back onto the cot. He appreciated Crane's offer for a night on the town and knew Crane's heart was in the right place over this veterinarian plan. He wished he could thank him but didn't know how.

"I'll call you when I nail something down with a vet," Crane said. He crouched down to exit through the secret attic door. Hendrix followed.

"I'm hungry," he heard Hendrix tell Crane. "Me, too," he heard Crane tell Hendrix.

Eggerton heard their muffled footsteps grow softer and softer as the two men made their way down the stairs.

He also heard a very distant, yet entirely audible, "I could flyyyyyy."

Then, he heard the front door of the house open and close.

Eggerton rushed over to the window and peered down at Crane and Hendrix as they exited the house. Eggerton found himself focusing on the top of Crane's head.

Yes! Crane was losing his hair. Eggerton could definitely see a bald spot growing on top of The Cranester's head. He saw an abundance of red freckles on Crane's thinning pate as well. Boy, Eggerton thought to

My Life With Wings

himself, Crane is sure going to look goofy when he loses his hair and all those freckles make themselves known. That made Eggerton laugh.

Crane and Hendrix walked down the flagstone path, away from Eggerton's home.

Suddenly, Hendrix waved his arms in a flying motion. He did it once. No more than that. Crane said, "Cut that out." Hendrix giggled again. Told Crane he was sooooo high and that he was ready to flyyyyyy. And then they climbed into Crane's car and left.

Later, at a bar, Crane and Hendrix had an argument. Hendrix left in a huff, but as soon as he exited the bar the burly linebacker encountered the head of his college's avian studies department and, a short time later, shared a heroin needle with her.

Chapter Thirteen

Eggerton sat back down on the cot. He had unfinished business. Crane and the linebacker had disturbed his sleep, Eggerton calculated, just prior to the 19-hour mark. No matter. Eggerton resolved to log in his sleep period at 19 hours.

What if the record is inaccurate from time to time? Who would know?

Eggerton had been dreaming when Crane woke him. Again, he concluded he dreamed the entire time he was asleep. Again, he dreamed just one dream.

He reached under the cot and retrieved the manila folder containing his notes from the morning he discovered his wings as well as his notes from his primitive airplane dream.

He selected the fly fishing catalogue envelope and wrote out in longhand the details from his second dream.

Here is what Eggerton wrote about his second dream:

I work in a circus and my best friend is a mouse. Not Mouse, my ex-wife, but a mouse. . .a real mouse. A little furry guy who shits little black balls. My little friend the mouse wears a red jacket and red hat and says "Fuck" a lot. "Fuck this and fuck that," my friend the mouse says.

The mouse doesn't say a lot, but when he does there is no questioning his meaning.

My job in the circus is to stand on top of a very high platform and jump off the platform when the mouse says jump. It's easy work, and each time I do it somebody gives me peanuts. I like peanuts. So does the mouse, although they make him fart. I always give him some of my peanuts. He farts and I pretend not to notice.

Each time I jump, I land in a net held below by some clowns. The clowns are not nice guys. They can be real assholes, especially a clown named Gus. I'll tell you more about him in a moment.

Anyway, getting back to our jobs, the mouse sits on my head and when I jump, he goes with me. The mouse and I have jumped off the platform three times and we have always landed in the net held by the clowns. But each time we jump, the platform seems higher.

The first time we jumped, the platform was 10 feet high. The second time we jumped, the platform was maybe 25 feet high. The third time we jumped, the platform was 50 feet high. When the mouse saw how high the platform was the last time, he said, "Fuck this." Actually, I think he said, "Fuck this fuckin' shit." He doesn't have much of a vocabulary, but what the fuck, he's just a mouse.

Anyway, today the platform is 100 feet high. My friend the mouse is speechless, he doesn't even say "Fuck this" when he sees how high the platform is. We climb up the pole to get to the platform; it seems to take forever because there has got to be a thousand or more rungs.

My legs grow weak as I climb, but there is an inner exhilaration that propels me up the pole.

My Life With Wings

Higher and higher I climb. Higher and higher. And higher still. Finally, we make it to the top.

The mouse is sitting on my head. He looks down and this time he says, "Fuck this." I look down. We are really, really high. I mean, really, really high. Below, the people in the audience look like little bugs. The clowns standing around the net below seem very, very far away. I can barely see their cheeks plastered with white makup, their fake plastic bulbous noses, the goofy clownish smiles painted across their faces.

As I said, one of the clowns is a jerk named Gus. I don't like him and I know he doesn't like me. The last time we jumped, as we flew off the platform, I glanced down and saw Gus. He was holding his hands up high, showing me he wasn't grasping the net. Still, the clowns who were doing their jobs, still holding the net, were able to sustain the force of our drop when we arrived at the bottom and nobody got hurt. But still, Gus let go of the net on purpose.

What can I say? There are a lot of assholes who work in circuses.

But my job is to jump off the platform. And so when the mouse says "Jump," I jump.

It feels as though the drop takes forever. We zoom down, the wind blowing by us as we cleave through the rowdy circus air that smells of too-sweet cotton candy and really rancid diarrheic shit that came out of Roscoe the Wonderhorse, who did his act right before us. I feel the G-forces pressing against my body, making it hard for me to breathe.

My lungs ache, but I force them to inhale and exhale, and that's how I stay alive while descending to the net below. On my head, the mouse is holding on tight, his little front paws clenching my brow. His grip is surprisingly strong, inasmuch as he's just a mouse. I think he's farting a lot up there, but they are not peanut farts, they are fright farts. I'm not sure, but as we're dropping I think I hear the mouse say, "Fuck this."

Still, the drop is an experience to behold. I have become unstuck by gravity, falling freely, parting the molecules as I hurtle down down down toward the net.

On the way down, we pass a flock of black birds circling around the pole that holds the platform aloft. One of the birds waves at us as we pass him. We exchange smiles. I wave back, but the mouse doesn't because he's holding onto my brow and farting.

Lord, I think, this is great. I find myself smiling widely and shrieking loudly, but I can barely hear my own voice because the crowd in the grandstand is cheering the mouse and me as we race to the finish.

"Whoooppppeeee!" I shout to the mouse.

"Fuck this!" the mouse shouts back.

As we approach the end of the flight I glance down and, once again, I see that Gus is not doing his job. He is not holding onto the net. Instead, he waves to me with both hands, an evil smile across his clowny face.

Finally, we hit bottom. Unfortunately, the mouse and I miss the net. Those bastards, the clowns, have pulled the net away from us at the very last second. I suspect that Gus might have had something to do with this. He is such an asshole.

Funny guys, I think.

Hee, hee.

We crash right into the hard surface of the circus ring. We leave a tremendous dent in the floor of the ring. As for the mouse and me, we are an ugly, bloody putrid mess. Broken bones. Smashed bodies. Pools of pus. Guts spread over the circus ring.

Children cry.

No peanuts for us.

Fuck that.

Eggerton read over the description of his dream several times. Again, it was hard for him to believe his dream took 19 hours to unfold, but he

My Life With Wings

was sure that it did. He thought hard for details he may have missed, but he couldn't think of any. He took the fly fishing envelope, which now contained the notes from his circus dream, and placed it in the manila folder along with his other notes, and then returned the manila folder to its place below the cot.

Chapter Fourteen

Eggerton let the phone ring a dozen times before finally answering. He had been in the secret attic room when he heard the first muffled rings from below. He let the first ring pass without rising from his cot. Next, he let the second ring pass. After the third ring, he stood and made his way out of the room, and then down the stairs to the kitchen on the first floor.

He could have saved himself time by stopping off on the second floor and picking up the extension in the bedroom, but he hadn't been in there since the first night of living with wings—which was, as he well remembered, a sleepless night.

He hadn't ventured into the bedroom since then, and he didn't mean to go back now.

So, by the time he made it all the way downstairs to the kitchen—and Eggerton was in no way imaginable in what anyone would call a hurry—the phone rang nine times. Eggerton lifted his hand to answer, but then paused, letting it ring a 10th time and then an 11th time. Finally, Eggerton decided to answer the phone on the 12th ring. He waited and waited and waited for what seemed like forever. "Ring, you bastard," Eggerton said out loud, then glanced around nervously to see if anybody heard. Of course, no one did.

Finally, the phone rang again. Eggerton, mildly surprised, answered.
"Hello?" he said.
"Hello," said a voice.
The voice asked to speak with Eggerton.
"Speaking," Eggerton said.

The voice identified itself as Meadowlark, the director of human resources at the newspaper. Eggerton knew Meadowlark. He was of average height, balding, 40 or perhaps 45 years old, nearsighted and partial to bow ties. It was an open secret at the newspaper that Meadowlark was still a virgin.

"How have you been?" Meadowlark asked.
"Not well," Eggerton said.

He decided there was no lie in that answer. Even though he truly did not have a head cold, he certainly couldn't state for the record that, physically, he was currently at his best.

"Well," Meadowlark said, "do you know you've been out of work eight days?"

Actually, Eggerton hadn't been aware of that. In all honesty, he lost track of time. In fact, he stopped calling in sick a few days ago. Frankly, he was a bit surprised anybody at the newspaper noticed his absence.

Eggerton was a subscriber to his own newspaper, but he hadn't read a single copy since he woke up with wings. Outside, the newspapers were piling up on the flagstone walk, left there faithfully each morning by the young boy who delivered them and who would, thirty years hence, be named president and CEO of a very important software company that would revolutionize the delivery of the US mail by adding an unprecedented five digits to the Zip Code.

(The new Zip Code, thanks to Eggerton's newspaper carrier, would be known as "Zip Plus Four Plus Five." Later, an additional adjustment to the process would result in a system know as "Zip Plus Four Plus Five Minus Three.")

Of course, Eggerton would not venture out to retrieve the papers. So, they accumulated, on the flagstone walk, piling up, each bundled tightly with a red rubber band twanged into place by the future software executive. Eggerton was sure, however, that the investment tables were being published right on schedule, and somebody from the copy desk was ably filling in, making up the pages in his absence and, perhaps, learning what Eggerton had known for years, which is the investment tables job on the copy desk is the best job on the copy desk if not the whole damned newspaper. And, in fact, if he had bothered to ask the boy who delivered the papers about the readability of the stock and bond pages he would have learned that yes, indeed, they were truly being published as accurately as before, and the kid should know because even at the age of twelve he read the financial pages, which did a lot to explain why he grew up to be very, very rich.

As for being absent eight days, well, that came as a surprise to Eggerton. He kept neither clock nor calendar in the secret attic room. He didn't know anything about astronomy, so he certainly couldn't tell time by the position of the sun as he gazed out the window in his secret room. And his sleeping schedule had been so haphazard lately that he certainly didn't know whether it was morning or afternoon. In fact, at the moment, he had no idea what time of day it was. He was about to ask Meadowlark if he wouldn't mind telling him the time, but he decided not to.

So, he said, "Eight days?"

"Look," Meadowlark said, "if you are truly ill, we want you to take all the time you need to recover. But the company rulebook says any employee out of work more than six consecutive days has to see a doctor. Have you been to see a doctor?"

Eggerton thought briefly of telling Meadowlark about how his friend Crane consulted with a number of physicians, including some of the city's most esteemed surgeons, and how Crane was now exploring veterinary science on his behalf. But also, Eggerton thought brightly to himself, Crane is—after all—a physical therapist, which is certainly not a doctor but nevertheless a professional in the medical arts.

He wondered whether an examination by a physical therapist would satisfy the company's rulebook. But then Eggerton reminded himself that Crane actually never did examine him, at least not in a medical sense. So, he knew it wouldn't do to tell Meadowlark he had been examined by a physical therapist because, in all actuality, he had not. And so, he told Meadowlark that he hadn't been to see a doctor which, he was sure, was the answer Meadowlark expected to hear.

"Well," Meadowlark said, "it is important for you to see a doctor. Do you have a doctor? Somebody you see regularly? We can give you a referral if you don't. We'll even make the appointment for you."

Eggerton said that wouldn't be necessary. He would see a doctor on his own.

"When you do that, the doctor has to send me a copy of his report. If he diagnoses an illness and thinks you need more time at home to recover, that's fine. The company allows you full pay for illness for three months, then you go on half pay for nine months. Do you understand that?"

Suddenly, Eggerton remembered that he had been practicing fake coughs and sneezes for several days. And there was no question that Meadowlark sounded skeptical—that it wasn't likely that the human resources director believed Eggerton was suffering from a bad cold.

Now was the time.

"Cufff," Eggerton said into the phone.

"What?" asked Meadowlark.

"Cufff," Eggerton repeated.

"Are you coughing?" Meadowlark asked.

"Uhh, yes," Eggerton said. "Pardon me."

And then, Eggerton said, "Chooo."

"What?" asked Meadowlark.

"Chooo," Eggerton said, again.

"And I suppose that was a sneeze?" Meadowlark asked.

"Yes," said Eggerton. "Pardon me."

And then Eggerton said, "Chooo."

"Another sneeze?" asked Meadowlark.

"Uhh, yes," said Eggerton.

He suspected Meadowlark wasn't buying any of it. All that work and effort he had put into developing a fake sneeze and a fake cough didn't seem to be working.

Still, he tried once more.

"Cufff...chooo," he said into the phone.

My Life With Wings

There was a long pause on the phone. Finally, Meadowlark told Eggerton that he needs to see a doctor, and the doctor needs to send a report on Eggerton's illness to the newspaper's human resouces department. And then he told Eggerton that he hoped he would soon feel better and could come back to work.

Eggerton hung up the phone without thanking Meadowlark for his concern.

Chapter Fifteen

Eggerton supposed, sooner or later, Mouse would show up. He heard the knock on the front door right after he broke the connection with Meadowlark. When he cracked open the door, he was quite shocked to see the face of his ex-wife. But there she was. His ex-wife. Mouse.

Eggerton said nothing.

"Hello," she said.

Mouse had a way of saying hello that beat the shit out of Eggerton every time. She always wore heavy red lipstick. Whenever she said hello, she would make an O with her mouth, and push the tip of her tongue nearly out of the O in a sort of scarlet piston-in-cylinder motion.

"Hello," she said again, pushing her piston nearly out of her cylinder.

Eggerton still said nothing.

"Hello," Mouse said again, really giving the piston all it was worth.

She smiled when she said it this time. It was a little half-smile. Eggerton knew that smile well. It beat the shit out of him every time.

"Aren't you going to open the door?" she asked.

He shook his head.

She pouted, one of those pouts that really beat the shit out of Eggerton.

"Why not?"

Finally, Eggerton spoke.

"Dun wanna."

Mouse was wearing jeans and a very baggy tank top. No bra, which was not unusual for her. Mouse had tiny breasts, which she preferred because they were low maintenance and she could go bra-less without attracting a lot of gawks from horny men. She wore very black sunglasses, which hid her hazel eyes. Mouse had curly red hair and fair, creamy skin and dimples in her cheeks. Her hands were jammed in her front jeans pockets, but her thumbs were exposed, jutting out in his direction. Her thumbnails were coated in a heavy, thick gloss of red nail polish. Mouse always paid a lot of attention to her nails.

Mouse wore a wide-brimmed sun hat made of enameled straw woven together in tight cross-hatchings. A red and blue ribbon was tied gaily around the crown, and the end of the ribbon dangled off the rear brim of the hat, hanging half-way down her back. Mouse was one of the few women Eggerton knew who could wear hats and not look silly in them. Mouse wore hats most of the time. Even indoors. He noticed she was barefoot, which wasn't unusual for Mouse. Mouse rarely wore shoes in the summertime. He stole a glimpse at her feet. Her toenails were painted in a hard red gloss.

"Well, I guess we can talk out here. Your friend Martin called. He said you were in trouble and that you might need my help. He wouldn't explain further. So, I came around to see for myself."

It was a lie. Mouse had been told by Martin that Eggerton was now sporting wings. Of course, Mouse found the story ludicrous. Still, she found herself curious and decided to drop in on her ex to see for herself.

Eggerton continued to keep the door open just a crack—just enough for his head to poke out. If he opened the door any wider, he knew Mouse would be able to see his wings. Certainly, at that point, he didn't know Mouse had already been told he had wings.

"Martin didn't say what the trouble was?"

My Life With Wings

Mouse shook her head.

"Can I come in?" she asked.

Eggerton said nothing for the next five seconds. He took the entire five seconds to debate what to do next. If he let her in, she would discover his wings. That, in itself, didn't trouble him: a lot of people knew about his wings—Martin, Woody, Crane, the stoned linebacker—although at the moment he regretted letting Martin in on the secret. He also regretted telling Crane as well, because Crane had brought the linebacker around. Eggerton regarded Hendrix as crude and boorish.

Still, Martin, Woody and Crane were all interested in his welfare and were trying to help, but he wasn't sure what Mouse could do. After all, Crane was seeking a medical cure; Woody brought the cot over and suggested a film script; Martin was anxious to sell the story to a book publisher. Eggerton supposed that if worse came to worse, and that he would have to spend the rest of his life with wings, it wouldn't hurt to have some extra money.

After all, he was quite certain Meadowlark was already drawing up the necessary papers to fire him, and so he was possibly looking at a future without a source of income.

And, frankly, he could not see himself standing in line at the local unemployment office to apply for benefits. Not wearing striped boxer shorts, certainly. And not with his wings fluttering behind, either.

And what would life be like living on the streets? It is tough enough for anyone to live on the streets, begging for handouts, but let's see a guy with wings try sleeping on park benches and begging for pennies. Eggerton closed his eyes and imagined himself homeless and living on the streets, and he knew it could never work for him.

And so, in truth, he was looking forward to whatever income a book deal or even a film script would provide.

But what could Mouse do to help him? He suspected that she did not know any book publishers or movie producers who would be interested in buying his story.

"Can I come in?" Mouse asked again.

"No," said Eggerton, rather abruptly.

But then he saw the change of expression of Mouse's face. Her expression changed from a sweet smile to a sorrowful frown.

And then she pouted again, one of those pouts that really beat the shit out of Eggerton.

And so he immediately changed his mind and said, "Yes, come in. Please come in."

Eggerton backed away from the door, leaving it open just a crack. Mouse followed him through the door. She opened the door wide, bathing the foyer with sunlight. Eggerton backed up further into the house, hiding in the shadows of the foyer. Mouse took off her dark sunglasses and looked around, inspecting the shelves of gewgaws by the front door, and the umbrella stand that looks like an elephant's foot set in place under the gewgaw shelves, and the framed ersatz Man Ray photograph hanging on the foyer wall and the hardwood floor, which was stained in a very, very dark walnut. It was the first time she had been in the house in a year. "You haven't changed much," she said.

Eggerton rolled his eyes back. Shows what she knows, he thought.

Mouse turned back to face him. At this point, finally, she noticed something queer. She raised her eyebrows. Pointed at him. Cocked her head to the right. Made that O motion with her mouth. Really started the piston going.

"Wings," she said.

"Yes," he said. "Wings."

It was true, Mouse said to herself, wings. My ex-husband has wings. Martin was not shitting me, after all. My ex-husband, Eggerton, is a winged copy editor. He makes the stock and bond tables come out right in the newspaper with wings.

During their time together, she occasionally found him boring; certainly, he was too bookish for her, and she abhorred that silly jazz he enjoyed, and had pestered him about spending so much money on the patio, arguing instead, and quite in vain, for an above-ground pool; and he was a lousy dancer who hated cruising the swing clubs while she, Mouse, fancied herself a high-stepper, and, above all, he really sucked as a lay.

(Do you believe, she recalled to herself, that he once fell asleep while in the throes of the act? That they were doing it, doggie style, he on his knees behind her, she on all fours just groovin' to the tune, and the next sound she heard was a deep, throaty snore and, looking back over her shoulder, couldn't help but notice the man whose head rested across the nape of her neck and who only a few seconds ago was making like a piston in a cylinder—yes, she thought of him in those terms as well—was actually and truthfully doing the ZZZZZZ act.)

All of that came back to her in a flash as she regarded his wings, but all of it was quickly forgotten as she wondered just why in the hell she had left him.

"You have wings," she said.

At Eggerton's suggestion, they retreated to the secret attic room—the only room in the house where he felt comfortable. "I didn't know this room was here," Mouse said, looking puzzled as she crawled through the passageway.

Eggerton sat on the cot. He was still wearing his boxer shorts; he still hadn't bathed since he woke up with wings. How long had it been now? Eggerton didn't have a notion.

Mouse sat on the floor, crossing her legs and leaning forward to rest an elbow on her knee. She made him go through the whole story. By now, he was weary of telling the tale, but Mouse insisted and the last thing Eggerton wanted was another fight with Mouse.

Mouse listened closely, adding a "Yes, I see" here and an "I can see that" there and an occasional "I agree." She nodded her head vigorously when he told her he was using a bad head cold for an excuse to stay out of work; she added a "That's a good idea" when he had fully explained the ruse. He was sure she was making those comments just to be nice and to feign interest in his plight. As for Eggerton, he left out a lot of parts. For example, he decided not to tell her about his dreams and hoped she wouldn't ask him about the manila folder, which was sitting in plain view under the cot. If queried about its contents, Eggerton decided, he would simply say, "Dunno, just a folder."

Still, Mouse learned virtually the whole story. He briefed her on Crane's efforts to seek a medical solution as well as Martin's suggestion to seek a book publisher. (Mouse didn't let on that she already knew about the search for a book deal.) Eggerton debated whether to tell her about Martin's suggestion that, for the purpose of Chapter Eight, they resume a conjugal husband-wife relationship; finally, though, he decided to tell her, and to tell her bluntly.

So he said: "Martin says we should fuck. He says it would make a better book. He says people are going to want to know what it's like to fuck a man with wings. What do you think of that idea, eh Mouse? Feeling like going at it right now? Eh?"

His heart beat rapidly as he spit out those words. He flushed. Eggerton was not, by nature, an aggressive or what you would call nasty person. Nevertheless, he was trying hard to shock Mouse, hoping she would say something on the order of "Hrrrumph," and then spin briskly on the forward ball of her right bare foot, and leave. Instead, Mouse stood, walked over and sat down next to Eggerton on the cot. She sat facing him; their eyes no more than inches apart. Eggerton became instantly aware of her odor: a deep, musky essence that he found soothing. It was a new odor; he hadn't recalled the scent during their uneasy months of marriage. She lifted her hand to his forehead and brushed a wisp of hair from his eyes.

"Is that what you want?"

It was.

But not for the purposes of literature. Yes, Eggerton wanted desperately to make love to Mouse. Yes, he was desperately lonely. Yes, he supposed he still loved her. Yes, he hadn't been to bed with a woman since she walked out on him a year ago. Yes, they never had what anyone would call an ideal, hold-each-other's-hands, smooch-in-the-dark marriage. Yes and yes, in the last days of their marriage, as the fighting and screaming and the sarcasm became ever more intense, Mouse had lashed out and struck Eggerton—hit him squarely in the jaw, drawing blood at the corner or his lip; but instead of hitting her back, he had been too shocked to react, and simply stared at her as she raged on and on and on but knowing, deep down, that it was over, this marriage of theirs.

Yes, yes, yes. All that was true. But yes, yes, yes, he sure did want to make love to her. Pump away at Mouse and make her squeak like a little tweety bird. Pistons! Cylinders! You betcha, yes. . .yes. . .yes.

So, Eggerton shrugged his shoulders. "Dunno," he said. He perspired heavily. Behind him, his feathers rippled silently. He saw Mouse glance quickly at his wings, then looked back into his eyes.

She placed her hands on his bare chest, then leaned forward and kissed him on the mouth, making that O formation with her lips. Eggerton returned the kiss. Seconds later, Mouse's jeans and tank top were

My Life With Wings

tossed into a pile on the floor, as were Eggerton's boxer shorts. Mouse kept her hat on, though, even holding onto it tightly with both hands as Eggerton nuzzled his face into her stomach. Strange behavior, thought Eggerton, but he was in no mood to question her on the issue.

In any event, Eggerton noticed a strong breeze during the act of coupling. Behind him, without his knowing it, his wings were flapping in great sweeping motions, stirring up the stale air in the secret attic room into broad yet invisible eddies and giving the lovers a warm, dry rushing whoosh across their naked, sweating asses.

The cot held up well. It shuddered under the weight of the lovers, to be sure, and the wooden joints creaked as Eggerton slammed his pelvis hard into Mouse, but there was no question that Clyde's Army-Navy Surplus Store carried durable, quality merchandise.

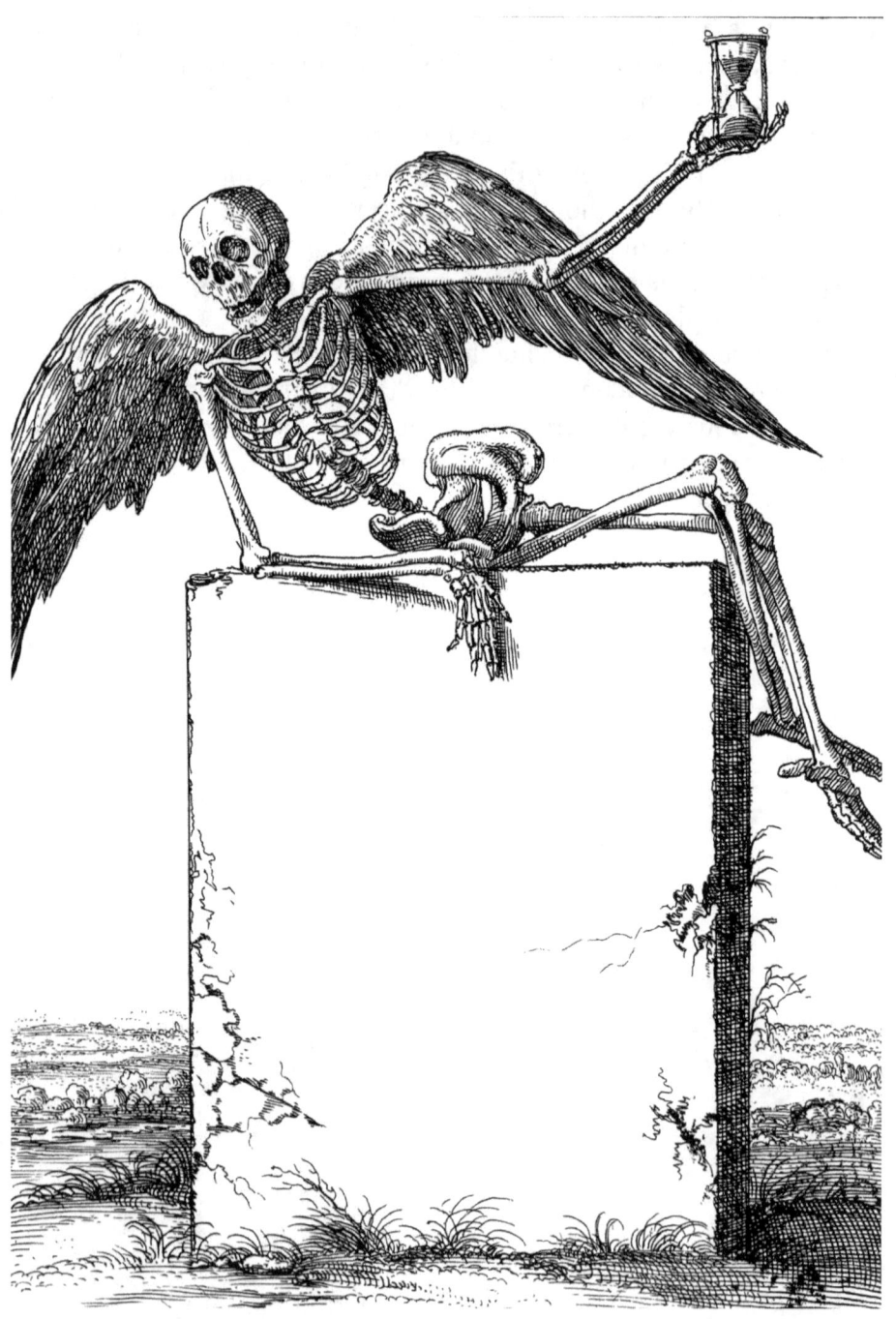

Chapter Sixteen

After sex, Eggerton dozed, face-down, on the cot. He slept for no more than an hour. He didn't dream. When he woke, he saw Mouse sitting on the floor, naked, cross-legged, her back bent slightly, grasping her toes, tiny breasts dangling. He thought it might be some sort of yoga pose. When Mouse and Eggerton lived together, Mouse spent a lot of time on her yoga mat. Among her favorite yoga poses was the crow, eagle, feathered peacock, firefly, heron, one-legged king pigeon and side-crane.

"Hello," said Eggerton.

She cocked her head to the right and smiled.

"Hello," Mouse said.

Eggerton sat up, stretched his arms over his head and fluttered his wings. He yawned. Glancing over at Mouse, he saw she was staring at him, a look of contentment on her face. She smiled broadly.

They talked. Mouse brought Eggerton up on her life—how she had rented an apartment across town and found a new job. She worked as a file clerk in the corporate headquarters of a major American poultry producer. She also maxed out her credit card and needed periodontal work but couldn't afford it. Her apartment was on the fifth floor of a mid-rise; it had one bedroom and a balcony where she raised potted plants and spent a lot of time drinking coffee, reading magazines and smoking thin, lavender-papered filtered cigarettes cleverly marketed to single women. She made an attempt at growing her own marijuana, but the plant died.

She also told him she dated occasionally but had not developed a relationship with any guy so far. In fact, over the course of the past year she had dated about a half-dozen times but never saw a guy more than once. All of the hookups, she said, had been through dating apps and none of them worked out.

Eggerton couldn't help but notice that she related these facts about her life with a certain air of gloominess. Eggerton concluded that Mouse's life had been somewhat dreary since their breakup. He found himself feeling sorry for her. Mouse was a young, vivacious woman. She enjoyed having fun and people enjoyed being with her. Sitting at home in a tiny apartment, drinking coffee, reading magazines. What kind of life was that for Mouse?

Finally, she asked him: "What are you going to do?"

"About what?"

"You know. . ."

"Oh," he said, "these." Meaning, of course, his wings.

Eggerton rubbed the back of his neck. He told Mouse he hadn't decided yet. The amputation option was still out there, even though Crane's search for a physician appeared to be bearing no fruit. Still, Eggerton supposed, all he really has to do is walk into a surgeon's office, any surgeon's office would do, and ask for an operation to remove his wings and, well, how does a doctor with any respect for his or her sacred oath to heal say no, be gone winged freak?

Eggerton and Mouse chewed that over for awhile and Mouse agreed that anytime Eggerton wanted them chopped off it would be easy enough to do. They also talked about the prospects for the book and maybe a Netflix deal. Eggerton said that if the book is optioned for a movie, he would want to be played by Ethan Hawke in the film version of his life. Actually, Eggerton vastly favored Joaquin Phoenix—he was by far the better actor, Eggerton thought. But Eggerton was a realist—a winged realist, to be sure, but a realist nonetheless—and knew that Phoenix was well past the stage of his career where he could pull off the portrayal of a misanthropic winged copy editor whereas Hawke, well, could wear the part like a glove and, in all likelihood, vie for an Oscar. Mouse nodded her head vigorously during this conversation, and Eggerton wondered to himself how he and Mouse failed the first time around.

At the end of the conversation, Mouse agreed to move back in with Eggerton. She dressed and said she would run back to her apartment for her clothes, and that she would return in a few hours.

Chapter Seventeen

After Mouse left, Eggerton retrieved the manila folder from beneath the cot. He selected the clean sheet of copy paper. He chose the clean sheet because he had a lot of information to record, and he knew he would use both sides of the page, easily. He did not have a new dream to write down; still, he had an idea he wished to sketch out. He decided to title the page: *The Land of the People With Wings*. Here is what he wrote:

The Land of the People With Wings
By Eggerton

Somewhere, perhaps in a land of high mountains or in the depths of a very thick and leafy jungle, exists a society of people with wings. The Land of the People With Wings is inaccessible to outsiders. If you don't have wings, you can't get in.

The homes are based on Greco-Roman architecture; they are made of stone and marble, and are high-ceilinged and very airy and comfortable. Inside, you won't find much furniture. In fact, just about the only furniture people keep in their homes are surplus Army cots.

Out front, great stone columns stand in front of the homes, and people sit on the plinths and talk among themselves whenever they have free time, which is quite often because in the Land of the People With Wings, nobody has to work. Food and other stuff you need are free. There is no such thing as money. In fact, they don't even have pockets sewn into their clothes.

People mostly dress in togas, which are designed to dip down low in back so the material doesn't snag on anybody's wings. A lot of the men go shirtless. A lot of the women go shirtless as well; in the Land of the People With Wings, public nudity is no big deal. Everybody goes naked whenever they want, but a lot of people feel the need to wear togas because they want to fit in with the architecture. They also wear sandals because it hurts to step barefoot on little pebbles.

Everybody's name is Greco-Roman as well. In the Land of the People With Wings, my name would be Eggertus. Also, in the Land of the People With Wings, my hair would be curly. Everybody's hair is curly there. Nobody wears glasses because everybody has good eyesight.

Everybody takes baths in public fountains that are in the middle of the city. The fountains feature a lot of Greco-Roman statuary: little cupids, centaurs drawing arrows into their bows, pan flute players, Venuses arching their backs so their tits protrude, that sort of thing.

Men and women meet and pair off as couples in the Land of the People With Wings much as they do elsewhere. They have weddings there, but the ceremonies are decidedly pagan. There is a lot of sacrificing of animals and drinking their blood as part of the ritual, but for the most part everybody has a good time. If you don't want to drink animal blood, you can drink wine. Nobody holds that against you.

My Life With Wings

Men and women have sex in the Land of the People With Wings much as they do elsewhere. Babies are born as babies, not eggs. I want to stress that again. Babies are born as babies, not eggs.

There is no disease in the Land of the People With Wings. There is no hunger. People with wings never have accidents and hurt themselves. Also, there is no crime. Nobody steals anything in the Land of the People With Wings. What is there to steal? Somebody else's toga?

Occasionally, people have arguments, but nobody stays angry with anybody very long. For the most part, everybody loves everybody in the Land of the People With Wings.

There is no electricity in the Land of the People With Wings. There is no technology. No computers, no television sets, no cars, no Internet, no microwave ovens, no stock market pages in the newspapers. No newspapers, either. People don't want electricity and technology. In the Land of the People With Wings, people just want to be left alone and not be bothered, so they can sit on plinths all day and talk to each other. That's what life in the Land of the People With Wings is all about. Sitting on plinths all day. They also drink a lot of coffee.

Eggerton read over his essay several times. He had used all of one side of the sheet of plain white copy paper and most of the second side. He liked what he had just written. In the days to come, as he sat alone in the secret attic room, he would page through the manila folder and read the story of the *Land of the People With Wings* many times, and take a lot of comfort in what he had written.

Chapter Eighteen

Mouse moved back in with Eggerton. Almost immediately, she gave him a sponge bath, making him stand in a basin while she cleansed his body by hand, toes to scalp, with a very expensive natural sponge she bought at a specialty bath shop. Mouse slowly worked the sponge as well as a soapy washcloth into each crevice, fold and crease in his body; she didn't find much in the way of actual dirt and grime, but after nearly two weeks of not bathing, the surface of Eggerton's body had taken on an oily, slick and sickly viscous consistency.

But she scrubbed hard, and Eggerton's skin soon responded by turning ruddy and supple. She playfully drew some flesh from his hip between a thumb and forefinger; he hooted in mock surprise, but let her tug away.

She was very careful while washing his back, because she had to work around his wings. While standing behind him, making circular motions with the sponge and washcloth around the small of his back, she paused to finger his wings ever so gently. She didn't know whether Eggerton had nerve endings in his wings and could feel her caress his feathers—and for one, brief second she seriously harbored the notion of plucking out a feather, but found herself chilled with gooseflesh at the thought and decided to leave well enough alone. And then, much to her surprise, he flapped his wings, making them swoosh back and forth…twice. She believed it to be an involuntary motion, and that she had somehow sparked the movement of Eggerton's wings by pressing a muscle or tweaking a bone, much the same way a doctor can make a patient's leg jerk by bonking a knee with a rubber mallet. As for her own reaction to the double-flap, the motion of Eggerton's wings took no more than two or three seconds, but soon after it was over she discovered a burning sensation as well as a wetness in her loins.

He turned around, catching her daydreaming.

He wanted to know whether the sponge bath was over.

"Umm, no," she said.

Mouse shuddered, then returned to work.

Next, she washed his scalp, squeezing the sponge over his head while working her fingers into his hair. He leaned his head back and closed his eyes. She could tell his hair had grown quite long; it now flopped over his ears and reached well down his neck. Later, she planned to comb it and, perhaps, even trim it.

Back around front she made him raise his arms so she could scour his armpits; then, she worked the sponge into his chest, puckishly tweaking a nipple and then, unable to help herself, she leaned into him and took his nipple between her teeth. He kissed the top of her head. She was touched by his display of affection. When they had been married, he would never have kissed the top of her head.

Finally, she gave him a shave. Since waking up and discovering he had grown wings Eggerton had certainly neglected his personal hygiene—there was no question about that. But he did make a few attempts at shaving the stubble off his chin, neck and cheeks. Eggerton spent a lot of time looking into his bathroom mirror—in fact, gazing at his reflection fifteen or twenty times a day—mostly checking to see whether his wings were still there. (They always were.) However, every time he gazed at his mirror image he did notice the stubble growing on his face, which bothered him. (Eggerton had, never in his life, grown a moustache or beard, finding facial hair not to his taste.) And so, he did shave a few times but by the time Mouse moved back in he hadn't shaved his facial hair in three days. And so Mouse found a fresh blade in a drawer of the bathroom vanity, lathered up Eggerton's face, and gave him a very gentle yet very pleasing shave. He enjoyed it so much he asked her to do it again.

"Maybe, tomorrow," she said.

Chapter Nineteen

Mouse prepared his food, cleaned the house and shopped for groceries. She couldn't convince him to move out of the secret attic room. He would come out for meals, taking breakfast, lunch and dinner in the kitchen, where he sat on a stool, allowing his wings to dangle behind him, while he ate off a plate that rested in his lap. After the meal, Eggerton deposited his plate in the kitchen sink and quickly returned to the attic room.

Mouse decided not to rush him—she knew coaxing Eggerton out into the world would take time and care. After all, if he did decide to go ahead with the book, there would be—*Lord!*—book signings in shopping malls, guest appearances on TV talk shows, interviews by newspaper reporters, photographers firing strobes in his face, whatever.

Mouse's life away from Eggerton had not been pleasant. The men she dated were asses, all of them interested in sex mostly. Certainly, Mouse enjoyed sex as much as any woman—indeed, she had a robust taste for coitus—but the romance just wasn't there with the guys she met and dated in her post-Eggerton life. In fact, she had been mulling over a reunion with Eggerton when Martin called and told her the strange little story about how her ex-husband had somehow sprouted a pair of wings.

"Wings?" she asked.

"That's right," Martin said.

"Wings?"

"Yes, wings."

Mouse had a habit of placing the eraser end of a pencil in her mouth when she was puzzled. In this case, she inserted the pencil in as far as the Dixon logo—nearly half-way to the point.

"When you say 'Wings,' what do you mean?" she asked Martin.

"I mean. . .wings."

Mouse wanted to know whether Martin meant the type of wings you would find growing out of birds.

"That's exactly what I mean. Wings, similar to what you would see on a bird."

"Oh," Mouse said, nibbling on the eraser.

Martin told Mouse the story of how Eggerton had grown wings, as it had been related to him. Then, Martin told Mouse that Eggerton didn't look well to him—he was thin and gaunt and jaundiced and dirty and had obviously not been eating well. He said Eggerton obviously needs somebody to take care of him. Martin was hoping Mouse would take the hint.

"It would be impossible," she said. "We were hardly on speaking terms when we split up."

Martin said he knew that. But Martin told her Eggerton agreed to a book deal—a bit of a lie, but Martin desperately needed Mouse's help—and Eggerton could stand to make a lot of money.

"How much?"

"Easily six figures, maybe more."

Mouse may have been broke, but she was not totally motivated by money here. She closed her eyes and imagined the dozens of newspaper and magazine stories, the network news stories, the podcasts, the Facebook and Instagram posts, the blogs and whatever, that were sure to be written about the Man With Wings. And somewhere, Mouse knew for certain, there was an enterprising journalist who would track down the former Mrs. Man With Wings.

My Life With Wings

The journalist would find her working in a mundane job, living in a tiny apartment, carrying credit card debt, bouncing checks, failing to make car payments, while her husband told his bizarre yet morally uplifting story to Stephen Colbert and *The New York Times* and was photographed in the 20-room seaside mansion he bought with the proceeds from the 20th printing of his book, and the magazine that ran the story—probably *People* or *Us* or *Entertainment Weekly*—would run a headline that would take advantage of her nickname and say something like "The Mouse Who Wouldn't Stand by Her Man" or words to that effect, and people would stop her on the street and say, "Aren't you Mouse?" and she would have to deny it and turn quickly away before they had an opportunity to say, "Yes, you are Mouse." And they would record videos of her running away and post them on Facebook and Twitter.

So, she told Martin that she would drop by to see what she could do for Eggerton, her ex-husband.

"Fabulous," Martin said.

"Yeah," Mouse said.

Chapter Twenty

Eggerton had been sleeping less and less and, as such, dreaming less and less. He blamed Mouse. She insisted on keeping him on a sleep-at-night, rise-in-the-morning schedule. No more sleeping for 18 or 20 hours at a time.

Oh, he still fell into a deep slumber the moment he flopped down on the cot, but now Mouse woke him roughly seven or eight hours later. And always in the middle of a dream.

That's what happened this morning. Right when the little guy with the beard was about to...about to...about to...what? Eggerton didn't know because Mouse shook him awake and told him to come down for breakfast.

"Yeah, sure," he grumbled as he sat up on the cot, stretching his arms, shoulders and wings.

Before heading down to the kitchen, Eggerton reached under the cot and withdrew his manila folder. Inside, he found his notes. He sifted through the loose pieces of paper for a moment, finally selecting the paycheck stub.

There wasn't much room to write on the back of the stub, to be sure, but Eggerton supposed it would do. After all, the dream had no ending—Mouse saw to that. Nevertheless, he found his pencil and recorded his incomplete dream. Here it is:

I'm flying high over the the middle of the ocean, somewhere. There is a lot of blue water below me in every direction. I have no cares, no worries. I feel free. I'm also not hungry. About an hour ago I spotted a school of herring darting through the clear water below. I flew down, snared one of the oily bastards in my beak and swallowed him whole. He squirmed a little on the way down but, boy, he tasted good.

And so, since I was in no particular hurry to find my next meal I spent time soaring as high as I dared go. Almost to the sun. Well, not quite that high. But you get the message. It was just a terrific time to be outdoors, high in the sky, riding the air currents.

And then I noticed a ship sailing below. There was no land in sight. No one onboard the ship seemed to mind, though. There is good weather and a gusty wind. I'm sure the crew will find their way home in good time.

Well, I'm minding my own business up in the sky when, suddenly, this little guy with a beard aboard the ship takes a bead on me and plunk, down I go. An arrow, right in my gut. Jeez, does that hurt. Next thing I know all these big guys are crowding around the little guy, giving him all kinds of hell. I would, too, but I don't know how to talk and, besides, I've got an arrow in the gut so I'm kind of concerned about that right now. I'm sure you can understand what that's like.

Anyway, one of the big guys, humongous bastard, hoists me up, ties a chain around my feet, and hangs me around the neck of the little guy with the beard. What a predicament! "Water, water everywhere," everyone keeps saying. I agree. There is water, water everywhere, but who gives a shit? Jeez, how did I get into this mess?

My Life With Wings

That's all Eggerton could recall from the dream. He supposed there could have been an end to that story, but he was at a loss to imagine what could have happened next.

"Coming for breakfast?" Mouse shouted from below.

"Yes, of course," Eggerton shouted back. On the way down the stairs, he wondered whether Mouse would be serving a cheese omelet again, and then his keen olfactory nerve told him, yes, she was, and that caused Eggerton to blanche, because he was sure growing weary of cheese omelets.

Chapter Twenty-one

Martin waited two weeks before calling Mouse. He wanted her to settle in, gain Eggerton's confidence, sell him on the idea of collaborating on a book. Oh, no question, the writing credit would go to Eggerton. Indeed, *My Life with Wings* would be Eggerton's book.

But Martin intended to write the book and receive a collaborator's credit, and—he intended to suggest—50 percent of the advance. He thought that was fair, even though his literary agent, a wiry, rambunctious raven-haired alcoholic named Junie Glaucous, told him to ask for less, perhaps 25 percent.

Martin would have none of it. He saw himself doing the work here: the interviewing, the writing, the revising—it would take months. Eggerton would simply be dictating his story and how much work could that be? No, Martin insisted to Junie, he wanted half. He assured Junie that Eggerton would take the deal.

In the meantime, he had a lot of work to do. He was, after all, deeply involved with his book on Bashful Bladder Syndrome. In fact, he dropped some sample chapters in the mail to Mouse and Eggerton. He felt that samples of his work would help sell them on the idea of MLWW, as Martin took to calling the project, with Eggerton.

"Did you receive the sample chapters on the BBS book I'm writing?" he asked Mouse.

He had taken to calling his Bashful Bladder Syndrome book by its initials, BBS.

"I believe so," said Mouse. "I know there is a bundle of papers around the house somewhere. I don't think Eggerton has seen them yet."

"Well, take a look at them," said Martin. "I think they'll give you some idea of the type of work I do. BBS is good. MLWW could be better."

Martin was, in fact, quite proud of his work on the BBS book. The chapters he sent Mouse were essentially transcriptions of interviews with BBS sufferers. He hoped Mouse would detect the sincerity and pathos in the interviews and come to understand he could do the same for Eggerton.

Here is a sample of Martin's work:

> *Question: Griffin, can you tell us about your experiences in public toilets?*
>
> *Griffin: Man, sometimes I gotta pee so bad but when I stand at the urinal it jus' won't come out, jus' won't come out, ya gotta know. Then, some dude'll stand next to me and he'll whip out 'is pecker and it's like goddamned Niagara Falls, like goddamned Niagara Falls, ya gotta know.*

True pathos, Martin thought.

"You should really take a look at those chapters," he told Mouse, "even if Eggerton isn't interested."

Mouse said she would try to have a look at them.

Martin wanted to know whether Eggerton was being more sociable.

"Not really," Mouse reported. "He rarely comes out of the attic. I've convinced him to take his meals in the kitchen, but he usually returns to the attic pretty quickly once the meal is done."

"What's he do up there all day?"

"Not much. He sleeps a lot. I think he stares out the window a lot.

On occasion, I've come up behind him while he has been standing at the window, and he hasn't noticed me."

"Does he read? Watch TV? Listen to music?"

Mouse told Martin that Eggerton has no TV or stereo in the attic, and whenever she's asked him if he would like a book or magazine he has turned her down. She did recall seeing him going through the papers in a manila folder he keeps under his cot.

"What's in the folder?"

"I don't know."

Martin suggested Mouse go through the folder if the opportunity presents itself.

Finally, Martin told Mouse he would want his literary agent to meet Eggerton.

Also, he thought, two or three publishing executives might sit in on the meeting as well.

Martin said his agent is talking about auctioning the book and it would help if the publishing companies could see the man with wings is no hoax.

Mouse said she didn't know whether that would be a good idea. But Martin persisted, and finally Mouse said she would bring up the matter with Eggerton but she certainly didn't want to promise he would agree to meet the executives.

Chapter Twenty-two

Mouse found the letter in the morning's mail. She opened the envelope, read the letter and debated with herself whether to show it to Eggerton. Her immediate reaction was to hide the letter, knowing that in his fragile mental state Eggerton was probably not up to digesting bad news.

Finally, she decided he should know the truth, so she climbed the stairs to the secret attic room. At least, she thought, when he reads the letter I will be with him to provide emotional support. When she wiggled in through the access door, she saw Eggerton reading through the pieces of paper in his manila folder.

He was so deep in concentration he hadn't noticed her entering the room. She stood, gazing down at him as he sat there, shirtless, his chest heaving in short but easy breaths.

"Lord," she thought to herself. "Why did I ever walk out on this guy?"

She watched him for several more minutes. Finally, she said, "Hello, honey. Whatcha doin'?"

Eggerton looked up quickly. He arranged the papers back in the folder and slipped it under the cot.

"What's in the folder?" she asked.

"Nothing," he said. "Just some stuff."

Mouse decided not to push it. But she did want to show him the letter. She handed it to him. It was from Meadowlark. It was addressed to Eggerton. It said:

> *As you may recall, we spoke regarding your illness approximately two weeks ago, and I advised you that, according to our company's illness policy, you are required to seek care from a medical professional who is then required to report his or her findings to me. Since I have not received a medical report regarding your condition, I have to assume you have not sought the care of a physician.*
>
> *If you have been to a physician and the doctor has failed to submit the required report, please call me immediately and I will contact the physician myself so we may discuss your case. If you have not been to a physician, I have no recourse than to terminate your employment, effective the end of this week. If you do not contact me by the end of the week, you should regard your employment at this company terminated. You can expect your final paycheck within seven days.*
>
> *It does not give me any pleasure to advise you of your pending termination, and I certainly hope you do take steps to contact a physician and seek proper care. After speaking with you on the phone I recognized symptons of acute respiratory distress —your continued and unabated coughing and sneezing. I am, therefore, convinced that your illness is genuine and that you are in need of professional medical care. But that is up to you. All I can do is urge you to follow our company's protocols and seek genuine medical care.*
>
> *Cordially,*
> *Meadowlark,*
> *director of human resources.*

My Life With Wings

"What should we do?" asked Mouse.

Eggerton said he would like another bath. Mouse said she was sure she could find the sponge.

Chapter Twenty-three

Mouse decided she would throw a party and invite a lot of people. Mostly, the party would be intended for Martin to convince Eggerton to agree to the book, and to introduce Eggerton to the publishing executives who Martin said would want to meet Eggerton and bid on his story.

She sat down with a pencil and a piece of paper—actually, the torn remnant of a brown grocery bag. Mouse never seemed to be able to find a piece of scrap paper in the house. She made a list of guests to invite.

Crane, of course. He would bring a friend, of course. Eggerton told her Crane had been keeping company with an obnoxious college kid named Hendrix as well as a little British birdie who liked to be called Duckie. Woody, of course.

And, certainly, Martin and his agent, Junie Glaucous. Junie told Martin that she felt she could interest three publishing company executives to attend the party, meet with Eggerton, and offer bids for the rights to his story.

Others?

Some people from the neighborhood. That nice Mrs. Hedron and that creepy Dr. Hitchcock. Why not? Mouse imagined them sitting off by themselves, drinking, and staying out of her way.

And some people from the newspaper. Even though Eggerton had been fired, he still had friends there: Somebody named Rhea? Isn't she a friend? Mouse could just call the paper and ask for Rhea on the copy desk.

Mouse counted up the names: Crane, Hendrix, Woody, Martin, Junie, the three birds from the publishing company, Mrs. Hedron, Dr. Hitchcock, Rhea. That would be eleven. Mouse and Eggerton would make thirteen. Not enough for a party.

She would ask Woody to bring some people from the restaurant where he worked. What was the name of that place? The Gleeful Goose? Or Goofy Goose? Something like that? Anyway, she knew Woody to be a gregarious fellow, someone who would have plenty of friends. She would talk to Woody and ask him to invite two or three people from his restaurant.

But that still wouldn't be enough people. Five or ten more bodies were needed. Mouse sucked hard on the pencil. She would tell Martin to find some people to come; the party was, after all, for his benefit. Surely he could draft some bodies. Hadn't he been meeting a lot of new people in public restrooms?

Mouse thought that if twenty or twenty-five people would show up, the party would take flight.

She wondered whether she should tell Eggerton about the plans for the party. Would it be a good idea to warn him that in a few days his house would be filled with twenty or twenty-five people, most of them strangers? Or just let everyone show up? Then, she would make her way up to the secret attic room and ask him to come downstairs. But he would be wearing his black and white striped boxer shorts and nothing else. And he may need a bath. And a shave.

But maybe that wouldn't be such a bad idea. After all, the publishing executives would see first-hand the story they were bidding to tell. On the other hand, what if they regarded him as little more than a dirty slob—a winged dirty slob, to be sure—but a dirty slob nonetheless.

Would his lack of proper attire and personal hygiene result in lower-than-expected bids?

There was a lot to ponder here. Indeed, Mouse concluded there was a lot about the publishing business she did not understand. She wondered whether she should call Martin or even Junie Glaucous and ask whether she should give Eggerton a bath before the party, but ultimately decided that was really an issue she should deal with on her own.

Chapter Twenty-four

Mouse wore a black Spandex miniskirt, tight black tank top, no bra, no stockings, but high-heeled sandals to make her legs look longer.

She owned a necklace composed of tiny white seashells strung together which fit tightly around her neck. As for a hat—Mouse could never really be without a hat—she chose a wide black ribbon tied around her forehead and knotted in back, resembling a pirate's headdress; not really a hat, per se, but close enough.

Red lipstick. Red gloss on her fingers and toes. A lot of costume jewelry rings. She stood in front of a full-length mirror and regarded herself. She approved. Mouse dressed this way because she knew she would have to help sell the book tonight.

Dr. Hitchcock was first to arrive, and he ogled her closely. Actually, he couldn't take his eyes off her tank top, and how the black fabric stuck snugly to her nipples. "How have you been?" he rasped, feigning an elegance she knew the dirty old doctor lacked. He let his tongue play over his lips.

Mouse saw his bad teeth.

He held her hand and gazed at her breasts. She felt naked in front of him. "Where is that husband of yours?" he asked. "I haven't seen him on the street lately. Has he been well? You know, if he isn't well, he should make an appointment and see me."

She mixed him a whiskey sour, planted his ass under the Cinzano umbrella on the patio, and told him she heard the doorbell ring, even though she hadn't. But she figured, rightly, the old fart was hard-of-hearing and wouldn't protest if she left him out here on his own while she ducked back into the house for no other reason than just to get away from him.

Actually, as she was making her way back into the house the doorbell did ring. It was Crane and that Hendrix kid. They were accompanied by a young woman with short black hair, dressed in a white hospital uniform. Crane told Mouse to call his new friend Duckie. "Hi," smiled Duckie,

Crane gave Mouse a warm hug and told her how well she looked. As usual, he was dressed in his white hospital uniform. Crane explained his clothes by telling her that he had come directly from work, which was a lie: Crane was on vacation and had only returned that afternoon from a week at the seashore where he and Duckie stayed in an aging and kitschy yet pleasantly air-conditioned motel. Their room had been decorated in a deep, seaside blue: the curtains were adorned with Warholesque renderings of seashells, the carpet a deep shag, the bedspread a light powder blue with a curious stain in the center. Crane supposed, accurately, that its origin had been menstrual.

Mostly, Crane and Duckie spent their time at the motel swimming pool—it had a diving board and a curlicue slide but was rarely used by the guests because it was rather tiny and kidney shaped and hardly conducive to serious swimming, although Duckie gave it a go, attempting to swim laps in the pool, a foolish endeavor given the pool's oddball shape. Crane made no such effort, which was perfectly understandable inasmuch as he never learned to swim and thought pool water uncomfortably cold.

He contented himself with lounging by poolside, wearing ever-so-brief Speedo trunks (white, of course), and admiring the body of his white bikini-clad British girlfriend. As the week wore on, and they both developed deep tans, Crane couldn't help but notice how pleasing their deep bronze skins contrasted against the white fabric of their swimwear. At night, Crane slept in white jockey shorts, one size too small, beneath a white sheet.

Mouse found Crane, Duckie and Hendrix some beers, told them the party was on the patio, and was about to show them outdoors when Woody let himself in through the front door. He was wearing a T-shirt identifying him as a member of the "Event Staff." It was yellow and the words "Event Staff" were stenciled in block letters across the front. As usual, his hairy belly hung through the crevice between the bottom of his T-shirt and top of his pants.

Oh, those pants. He wore cutoff shorts cut off too short for a man of Woody's girth. His flabby thighs poured out from the leg holes of the shorts, which fit too snugly over his crotch, surely compressing his testicles.

Mouse wondered whether the cutoffs were actually painful.

Woody also wore black Chuck Taylor high-top sneakers which were, apparently, right out of the box. Not a scuff on them. The laces were still puffy and starched white, the aluminum eyelets still polished as shiny as the chrome on a hotrod. No socks, though, or if he was wearing socks, they had bunched up below his heels. All in all, Woody looked fairly ridiculous.

"Howzit?" Woody asked.

"Howzit?" Crane answered.

They gave one another the high-five.

Mouse screwed up her face. Birds of a feather, she concluded.

Hendrix produced a joint.

"Time to get high," he said.

Crane furrowed his brow.

"Is that all you think about?"

"Where's the fucker with the wings?" Hendrix asked, as he struck a match.

"Shut up," said Crane.

"Wings?" asked Duckie. "Do you mean spicy wings? I looooovve those. They make my tongue tingle."

Throughout this banter, Mouse couldn't help but notice Woody hadn't come alone. He was accompanied by a tall young man with shoulder-length hair, an earring, a nose ring, a thick notebook under his arm, a downy mustache above his lip, a pencil behind his right ear, a pair of translucent-red John Lennon-inspired sunglasses perched atop his nose and, Mouse observed, a canker sore on his lip. He also wore an "Event Staff" T-shirt. Unlike Woody, though, the young man had taken a pair of pinking shears to his T-shirt and trimmed off fabric from the midsection exposing a hairless, yet lean, belly. Mouse could tell he used pinking shears because the new hem of the shirt hung across his ribs in a sawtooth pattern. Woody's friend sported a tattoo of a rising sun inked into the area around his navel. The sun had a wide-eyed, astonished expression, its mouth a gaping "O." The young man's navel took the place of the "O."

Getting back, for the moment, to that T-shirt, apparently Woody and his friend had just come from the same "Event" where they had been members of the "Staff," working together in crowd control; or perhaps they stood at the gate taking tickets or, perhaps, they simply helped clean up. But whatever their jobs may have been, Woody was never prompted by Mouse or Crane or Hendrix (who was by now toking heavily on his marijuana) to tell them exactly which "Event" they may have been drafted to "Staff."

"This is Evan," said Woody. "He's a screenwriting student. He's going to write the film script."

"Yeah," said Evan.

Woody explained Evan held a part-time job at the Happy Buffalo Wing. Woody, grasping Evan's shoulder in a firm yet brotherly manner, confided to all that Evan is one of his best deep fry guys.

Hendrix looked up. He had just taken a long draw on his joint and was now letting the smoke escape from his mouth, where he quickly aspirated it back into his nose.

"Yo, dude!" he said to Evan.

"Yo, dude," said Evan.

"Do you two know each other?" asked Crane.

They did. They had taken an ornithology class together. Hendrix came close to failing the class, but managed to earn a passing grade

My Life With Wings

when he permitted himself to be seduced by the professor, a recently-widowed 51-year-old cougar who had been coming on to him since the start of the semester.

Hendrix picked up the signals early, to be sure, but held off her advances at first knowing he would likely do little to no work in the class and would, therefore, withhold his carnal favors from the professor until he could expect something in return. When, finally, he did submit to his professor's advances she told him, "Don't get any ideas, this is all about the sex."

"Uhh, yeah," he said, all the time laughing on the inside for he knew much better than she did that it wasn't at all about the sex it was all about Hendrix maintaining a 2.0 GPA so he could keep his scholarship and continue playing football. And, ultimately, the cougar awarded him a grade in Ornithology 101 that did enable him to maintain his 2.0 GPA.

Evan barely passed the class himself, managing to eke out an acceptable grade on his own although, even Evan would readily admit, he had no future in ornithology.

They compared notes on the class briefly.

"What a bitch," said Hendrix.

"Yeah, a bitch," said Evan.

"Wanna get high?" asked Hendrix.

"Yeah," said Evan.

Hendrix passed the joint to Evan, who drew hard on it.

"Wait until you see this fucker with the wings," said Hendrix, with a giggle.

"Wow," said Evan.

At that point, Mouse decided to push them all out to the patio, where they could keep Dr. Hitchcock company. She retrieved some beers from the kitchen and led them through the back screen door, holding one beer over her head as the others followed, as though they were goslings following a mama goose to the pond.

Chapter Twenty-five

Eggerton woke suddenly when he heard the front door open and close and then Woody's muffled voice. He quickly sat up and reached under the cot for the manila folder. He found his pencil, then rifled through the pages in the folder until he found the receipt from Clyde's Army Navy Surplus Store.

There had been a new dream.

He felt a chill. He shuddered. He swallowed hard.

He checked his wristwatch, noting the time on the back of the receipt from Clyde's. It was 4:14 p.m.

Chapter Twenty-six

The party was turning out to be a roaring success. After Woody, Evan, Crane and Hendrix joined the doctor on the terra cotta patio, other guests soon arrived. Indeed, there were more guests than Mouse expected. She worried about running out of food and drinks.

Mouse picked the music for party, spending hours sifting through Eggerton's CD collection. Of course, Eggerton owned a lot of jazz recordings. Mouse found some sweet but sullen music by Bird Parker, and that seemed to put the guests at ease.

Rhea showed up with her new boyfriend, Meadowlark—the human resources director at the newspaper who had just fired Eggerton. Mouse saw that Rhea was a short and chubby woman with a complexion problem, curly brown hair, chapped lips and dirty fingernails. Meadowlark was tall, thin and fastidious; he wore a white long-sleeved shirt, gold cufflinks, no jacket, a red clip-on bow tie and suspenders.

Rhea and Meadowlark approached Mouse on the backyard patio. She giggled a hello. Mouse could tell she was already slightly drunk. "How's Eggerton?" she asked. "We miss him down at work. I've had to put together the stock and bond tables since he's been gone. I hope he comes back. I really hate that fuckin' job. I want to get back to the sports pages." Rhea held a lit, unfiltered cigarette between her fingers as she spoke. She inhaled deeply after speaking then blew a blue cloud of rancid smoke skyward.

Mouse returned the comment with a half-smile. She glanced at Meadowlark, wondering if he was able to absorb the mental message she had hoped to transmit to Rhea: *"Ask this asshole of a boyfriend of yours when Eggerton is coming back to work. After all, he just fired him."*

Mouse turned toward Meadowlark. She noticed that his shirt was composed of a very thin fabric and that he wore a white cotton V-neck T-shirt underneath. She saw that his belt was buckled very tightly and wondered whether he was was in some measure of discomfort. She also noticed that Meadowlark had something of a dandruff problem. She saw numerous tiny white flakes of dead skin sitting atop his scalp.

Mouse debated with herself the notion of asking Meadowlark why he would come to a party at the home of an employee he just fired, but soon decided to let the matter pass. Why ruin a good party? But then Meadowlark spoke and said that if he had a chance to talk with Eggerton and hear his explanation for missing all that work, and if there is an acceptable reason for his absence—well, maybe, he might be able to rescind the termination.

"You know," he said, "when I spoke with him on the telephone he sounded terrible. Raspy cough, persistent sneezes. I'm no doctor, but I can tell a respiratory infection when I hear one."

Mouse suddenly realized that she had misjudged Meadowlark. He really wasn't that bad of a fellow, after all. She told him that she thought it was terribly kind of him to make the offer and she promised to find some time for Meadowlark to sit down with Eggerton.

And then she remembered Eggerton was sporting wings these days and, well, Meadowlark would probably be able to draw his own conclusions with or without a discussion once Eggerton decided to make an appearance at the party.

My Life With Wings

Yes, what about that appearance at the party? She glanced back toward the house and decided it was time to track down her ex-husband in his secret attic nest and tell him to get his feathers downstairs and meet the guests. She started making her way to the house when she felt a tug on her arm. She turned to find a tall, thin woman smiling at her through over-glossed lips.

Mouse never saw her before and, certainly, didn't remember letting her into the house. She guessed the woman was at least 60 or 65 years old. Her skin was pasty white, her hair an obvious dye job. The woman had, in fact, dyed it a deep, blue-black shade. Her eyebrows were tweezed, and she had yellow teeth. Too much smoking, Mouse supposed.

She wore a black jersey with floppy sleeves, black satin pajama pants, black pumps and no stockings. Her ankles were rather bony and, Mouse noticed, terribly scabbed. She wore a lot of costume jewelry: large onyx-colored hoop earrings; garish, obscenely large rings on each finger, a dozen or so needle-thin gold and silver bracelets dangling loosely from her wrists.

She took Mouse's hand firmly in her hand and pumped it vigorously, jangling her bracelets. Mouse nearly said "Ouch!" because the woman's grip was so strong.

"Junie Glaucous," the woman said. "You must be Mary Ann Eggerton."

"Oh! Of course!" Mouse said, her hand still in Junie's grip. "You're Martin's friend. Is he here?"

"No, he's coming on his own," Junie said while continuing to hold Mouse's hand. "I'm sure he'll be along any moment."

Junie peered into Mouse's eyes. Mouse found her gaze icy and insincere. She felt nervous and vulnerable—as women frequently do when they suspect men are undressing them with their eyes. A very slight dizzy spell passed through Mouse's body. She shook off the vertigo very quickly but wondered why she felt so out of sorts.

For the longest of all moments, Mouse and Junie stood silently, side by side. Junie absolutely refused to let go of Mouse's hand. She smiled broadly through her red lips and yellow teeth and stared hard into Mouse's face while Mouse stood dumbfounded, unable to conjure up a single word that would indicate to the woman that she should release her hand. Mouse noticed that not only did Junie have the grip of a Sumo wrestler, but her hand was cold and damp. It was most unpleasant.

Mouse decided to smile through the unpleasantness. Junie could mean a lot to the success of the book.

Mouse wondered whether she should make conversation. Perhaps if she could engage Junie in a chat of some sort, she might get caught up in the topic and unconsciously release Mouse's hand. But Mouse could not come up with a topic that she thought might prompt a response from Junie. The weather? Did she see some movie that might be playing at the local cinema? Read any good books lately? Did you see that item in the news? None of it seemed to make sense to Mouse.

Finally, Mouse said, "Is that the door? Maybe that's Martin now."

There had been no knock on the door. Mouse hoped Junie would believe the lie, releasing Mouse from her vice-like grip so she could answer the door.

Junie did turn her head toward the door but didn't release Mouse's hand.

"Let's have a look," Junie said. She spun on her heel and commenced traipsing back through the house, heading for the door, yanking Mouse along behind her. She had a gait strikingly similar to one of those stilt-walking guys who dress up like Uncle Sam.

Mouse wanted to stop, plant her feet firmly and yank her hand away from Junie. Then, she wanted to kick Junie in the shins, knock her to the floor and press her stiletto heel into Junie's throat.

She envisioned herself grinding her heel as Junie gagged with pain, choking as she swallowed her own tongue. She wanted to see blood come out of Junie's nose. She wanted to see Junie's face turn purple. She wanted to hear Junie sputter her last breath.

Mouse wanted to do all that before Junie made it to the front door because Mouse knew full well nobody was at the front door. Obviously, it was going to get a little embarrassing when Junie flung open the front door and discovered nobody standing at the end of the flagstone path. Mouse suddenly felt an urge to urinate.

They were at the front door. Junie, seemingly gripping Mouse's hand tighter now than ever, opened the front door.

My Life With Wings

"Martin. . .it is you!" Junie squealed.

Incredibly, Martin stood outside, his feet planted firmly on the flagstone path. He drew heavily on a cigarette, letting the smoke escape lazily from his nose. He flicked the ashes from the butt.

"Junie, you old crone!" he laughed.

Junie shrieked with delight.

Martin leaned over and hugged Junie. She responded by putting her right arm around his shoulders. She continued to hold Mouse prisoner with her left hand.

"Come in," Mouse said. "Can I get you a drink?"

Mouse hoped Junie would let go of her hand then. Obviously, Mouse would need two hands to mix a drink.

"Maybe later," Martin said.

Mouse winced.

Chapter Twenty-seven

Eggerton pushed open the window in the secret attic room and leaned out. Below, he could see Martin standing at the door, his balding pate reflecting the sunlight.

He also noticed a bit of commotion. A loud and flamboyant woman dressed entirely in black took a step out of the house, waving her arms. And clenched tightly in one of her hands was the hand of someone else. Was that Mouse?

Eggerton turned to look skyward. The sun was very bright this afternoon, the cloudless sky very blue, the atmosphere mostly a sweet aroma of fresh leaves but—Eggerton could tell—just the slightest bit pungent from a jet contrail Eggerton could see, oh, perhaps thirty or forty miles to the south. He let his head swivel on his shoulders.

Suddenly, Eggerton's eyes were drawn to the pitch of the roof. He wondered about it. The roof was steep, to be sure, but not terribly steep.

Eggerton heard some voices. He glanced down again. Martin was speaking with that woman in black; then, they each stepped into the house and were now gone from Eggerton's view.

Eggerton took a step away from the window and looked down at himself. He was still wearing his black and white striped boxer shorts. They weren't quite as soiled as they had been—Mouse had laundered them a few times—but Eggerton decided they were the only clothes he felt comfortable wearing.

He was barefoot. No shirt. Mouse had given him a sponge bath that morning, so he was clean. She also shaved him. He brought his hand up absently to feel the smoothness of his cheek. After the shave and the sponge bath, Mouse made him promise to wear a pair of dress slacks for the party that afternoon. She brought up a freshly-pressed pair of gray cotton Dockers that had been hanging in his closet as well as some socks and shoes, which she shined to a hard gloss. She also brought along a fresh pair of boxer undershorts. She didn't bring a shirt, of course. There was no way he could fit into a shirt. When she dropped off the clothes, she told him that in time they could consult a tailor who, she felt, could design some type of upper torso garment Eggerton would be able to wear.

She placed the garments on the cot, and said she had to run some errands before the party. She kissed him lightly on the lips, told him to dress, and promised to be back in an hour. When she left, Eggerton picked up the clothes, folded them carefully and deposited them in a corner of the secret attic room. He sat himself gently down on the cot, retrieved the manila folder and read through his notes carefully. Soon, he felt drowsy. He put his face down into the canvas of the cot and fell asleep.

That's when he had his final dream on the cot.

Now, fully awake, he stoood at the window of the secret attic room. And now, for the first time in weeks—perhaps for the first time since that remarkable day when he woke up to discover that he had grown wings—he couldn't help but feel good about himself. Eggerton felt as though he had reached a turning point in his life.

Eggerton decided he didn't want his wings amputated, that he enjoyed wings and if forced to live with them for the rest of his life, well, so be it. People have lived with all sorts of maladies—physical deformities, diseases, mental incapacities—and Eggerton supposed he could live a useful life and even edit the stock market tables with wings.

My Life With Wings

But as Eggerton continued to ponder the matter he found himself wondering why he had always looked at his wings as a malady. Were they really a physical deformity? No, not at all. They were a part of his body, a part of his soul. As much a part of him as his toenails, his morning stubble, his armpit hair, or any other part of his body.

Eggerton's attention was drawn back to the roof.

He remembered that he had never been on the roof of his own house. Until now, he never had a reason.

Chapter Twenty-eight

"Are they here yet?" Martin asked. "Yes, yes," Junie said. "All three are here."

"All three?" Martin asked, obviously impressed. "Yes, yes," Junie said. "All three. Can you believe it?"

She squealed, hugged Martin and squeezed Mouse's hand, bringing it to her sagging, aging, withered but quivering-with-breathless-anticipation breasts.

Mouse had no idea what these two were talking about. She wished only that Junie Glaucous would release her grip. It was beyond uncomfortable now. And the urge to urinate had now become quite intense.

Mouse closed her eyes and imagined herself on a deserted island, nude, running gaily through the sand dunes, her body bronzing slowly in the tropical sun, lotus blossoms adorning her hair, no clammy old half-drunken hag holding her hand.

She opened her eyes and said, "Please, would you mind letting go of my hand?"

Junie didn't hear the plea. She had been whispering in Martin's ear. He giggled, then whispered back in Junie's ear. She giggled.

Mouse repeated her request. Junie turned to face her for not more than a second, clearly unsure of what Mouse just said. She shrugged, then returned to her conversation with Martin, oblivious to the pain and loathing she engendered in Mouse.

Mouse was about to make her request a third time when Junie and Martin agreed it was time to meet the "three." She felt a tug on her hand as Junie yanked her toward the rear of the house. She had no choice but to follow. Her boiling bladder felt ready to explode.

Junie led them to the terra cotta patio. Three men stood awkwardly side by side, drinks in their hands. Mouse hadn't noticed them before. They were dressed in dark suits, white shirts and conservative ties. Junie strode over to them, Mouse in tow. Martin quickly followed.

"Gentleman!" Junie gushed. "So good to see you!"

They all smiled politely. Junie introduced each man to Mouse and Martin. They were the three publishing company executives Junie invited to the party to meet Eggerton and make bids on the book.

The first man was quite tall and quite bald; he had a hooked nose and a pencil-thin black moustache and the type of eyebrows that met just above the bridge of his nose, forming a wide black line across his face. Clearly, Mouse thought, the symmetry of his face was all askew: thin mustache below the nose, thick eyebrows above the nose. "Simon," Junie smiled. "How have you been, you old bastard! Everyone, this is Simon Cuervo."

Simon smiled broadly. "Junie, you old whore," he said. "How the fuck are you?"

The second man was short and sturdy with close-trimmed brown hair and a pink, hypertensive complexion. Perspiration dotted his ruddy, lined forehead. His ears were rather large. And they were hairy, too. And Mouse noticed stringy, unkempt hairs dangling from his nostrils. "George," Junie said. "Still having sex with your sister?" George laughed at the comment, and Mouse wasn't sure whether Junie was being serious. "Oh, Junie, you bitch. Anytime you want to bang, let me know." Junie yanked on Mouse's hand and said, "Everyone, this is George Le Coq. And believe me, he sucks cock!" George delivered a hearty belly laugh. Mouse also thought she heard a fart and then decided from a newly-detected rancid odor that it was true, Mr. La Coq did just lay a fart. "Oh, Junie," George said. "You are such a piece of shit."

Junie and George then shared a hearty laugh.

The third man was quite rotund. He wore a professorial beard and was enjoying a bloody mary, which Mouse noticed was dribbling onto his beard. He was extremely well-tailored, yet occasionally wiped the saucy red drink from his beard with a sleeve. Mouse could see his teeth needed straightening.

"Donny, Donny, Donny," Junie said. "How ya bangin' 'em?"

Donny seemed to have something of a more sedate personality than the other two. "OK," Donny said. "I'm well. And you?"

"Just fine," June said. "Everyone, this is Donny Passero."

They made small talk. Mouse noticed Simon leaning toward her, looking hard at her breasts. George was interested in the progress of Martin's BBS book. Donny seemed disinterested in the whole affair. She observed that quite frequently, Donny glanced at his watch.

Junie was still holding Mouse's hand, although not quite so tightly. Mouse thought she could break away now by simply snapping her hand back and was about to do so when George related a strange but humorous publishing company-insider anecdote about how the grandson of the founder just paid $1 million to a manga artist from Japan to produce a graphic novel about a Belgian situation comedy star with a gambling addiction, and how the whole publishing industry was laughing hysterically at this goofy deal. The story made Junie squeal, which made Junie tighten her grip again. Which caused a rush of air to escape painfully from Mouse's lungs.

Mouse wanted to pee so badly, the only thought that held her back from releasing at that very moment was the notion that creating a puddle of sweet honey-ocher urine at the feet of a group of publishing executives was no way to commence a literary auction.

Chapter Twenty-nine

Eggerton folded his wings tightly into his body. Then, he backed toward the window in the secret attic room and sat down on the sill. Next, he drew his knees in close and planted his heels on the sill. Now, it was all about to get very tricky.

He grasped the underside of the top of the frame with his fingers, waited until he was sure his grip was firm and true, and hoisted himself into an erect position. He was now standing on the windowsill, his body outside the window, but his hands still holding the upper frame.

His next job would be to transfer his hands from the window frame to the roof. The gutter was about chest high and obviously the place to move his hands.

But he fretted the gutter would pull away from the roof if he transferred his weight to it. The gutter was in all likelihood as old as the house; if the nails were rusty they would pull out easily.

And yet, he had no other choice. There were no other hand-holds available. Above the gutter were the slate tiles; he knew that if he grasped the tiles instead of the gutter it was possible they would pull right off the roof. So, the gutter was his only choice.

He closed his eyes. Took a deep breath. Worked up the nerve. Opened his eyes.

Eggerton released his grip from the upper frame and brought his hands quickly to the gutter, gripping the lip of the old tin channel with his fingers. He continued to let his feet support most of his weight. Slowly, he transferred his weight to his hands, testing the anchoring on the gutter second by second.

Finally, Eggerton concluded the gutter would support his weight. He allowed himself to relax.

But not for too long. Now, Eggerton faced the most challenging leg of the adventure. He planned to rest his palms flat on the first row of slate tiles, then hoist himself up—using only the strength in his arms—until he was high enough to plant a knee on the roof.

Eggerton knew he would be asking a lot of his body. Eggerton was not a particularly athletic person. Suddenly, his last dream, which had snaked its way through his slumbering psyche just a short time ago, made its way back into his brain. This time, his dream had not been a a fantasy: No jumping into circus nets with foul-mouthed mice, no taking an arrow in the gut from a sharpshooting seaman, no bumpy ride aboard the world's first airplane. No, this time his dream recounted a very real experience from long ago. It happened in high school. Yes, high school. Gym class.

Gym class.

Mr. Bunting, the gym teacher. A former Atlanta Falcon. The gymnasium was equipped with three heavy ropes bolted to the ceiling, side-by-side by side-by-side. The distance from bottom to top was about fifty feet. Everybody was required to climb a rope. To pass rope-climbing, you had to make it to the ceiling employing the hand-over-hand technique, although you could use your feet as well.

The technique required the climber to lock the rope into the instep of one foot by pressing down on it with the heel of the opposite foot. In the vernacular of the rappeller, the technique is known as lock-and-lift.

My Life With Wings

Successfully ascending to the ceiling by using the lock-and-lift technique, Mr. Bunting informed the class, is awarded with a grade of C.

Mr. Bunting instructed the class to gather around the ropes. Eggerton fell into the crowd. He always felt uncomfortable and self-conscious in his gym clothes—white T-shirt and white shorts, white socks and black, low-cut sneakers. He knew his skinny body and sunken chest hardly filled out the T-shirt and shorts. Also, the gym was always cold and gave him bumpy gooseflesh.

Mr. Bunting grasped the center rope and started making his way toward the ceiling.

"Lock...lift...lock...lift," Mr. Bunting said while demonstrating, as he hoisted himself up about eight feet from the mat.

Mr. Bunting was quite the physical specimen. He had blown out a knee while chasing down O.J. Simpson on a kick return in a pre-season game. Still, Mr. Bunting had been little more than a journeyman pro, bouncing from team to team in a career that had somehow lasted four seasons.

The play in question occurred in the final quarter of the final pre-season game; indeed, just before halftime, the Falcons' coach had decided to cut Mr. Bunting from the roster.

So, Mr. Bunting's injury turned out to be quite fortuitous; instead of cutting Mr. Bunting—the league rules prevented a team from releasing an injured player—the Falcons placed him on their team's injured list, which meant he could collect a full salary for the year even though his career was over. After his knee healed, Mr. Bunting found a job as a high school gym teacher.

After demonstrating lock-and-lift Mr. Bunting let himself slide down to the mat. Next, he demonstrated how one could achieve the grade of B on the rope climb. Using the muscles in his shoulders and biceps but letting his feet dangle loosely below him, Mr. Bunting hoisted himself up a dozen feet, going slowly hand over hand.

When he had gone as far as he thought necessary for purposes of demonstration, he stopped and let himself slide down to the mat again.

Mr. Bunting was hardly winded.

He wore a blue polo shirt that fit snugly over his torso. The muscles in his arms, flushed with blood, stood out, giving his shoulders a round, cannon-ball appearance.

Mr. Bunting adjusted his polo shirt, which had become unhitched from his slacks, and said he would now demonstrate how to achieve an A.

He hoisted himself onto the rope, then lifted his midsection into a 45-degree angle, allowing the rope to dangle between his legs. And then, he climbed the rope in the hand-over-hand technique, but keeping his midsection bent, his legs in the pike position, the toes of his black, ripple-soled athletic shoes pointed. This time, though, he didn't stop a dozen feet off the floor, but made his way all the way to the top; finally, he released one hand from the rope and touched the ceiling.

"This gets you an A!" he shouted down to the boys standing around the mat. Most of the boys stared at Mr. Bunting, impressed with his skill and sheer muscular strength. Two boys who did not bother to look were a pair of future convenience store workers named Booby and Turk, who were making arrangements to get high after school and had, in fact, secreted marijuana cigarettes in their threadbare sweat socks.

Mr. Bunting slid down the rope. Again, he was hardly winded.

The boys formed three lines. Eggerton fell in the middle somewhere. A few of the boys were able to achieve the A, making it all the way to the top in the pike position. Some boys climbed the rope with their feet dangling, accepting the B but knowing with some practice and perhaps a shot at the rope next year, the grade of A was certainly not out of the question.

Most boys were simply satisfied with the lock-and-lift method, Booby and Turk among them; indeed, after each lock-and-lift climber completed his mission to the top and returned, Mr.

My Life With Wings

Bunting would nod approvingly and make a mark on his clipboard, satisfied that he had brought some measure of achievement to the lives of these boys, and that if they ever found themselves at, well. . .the ends of their ropes. . .that he was responsible for showing them how to rescue themselves from their predicaments by using the always reliable lock-and-lift method. Even watching Booby and Turk make their ways up the ropes, and knowing full well the two boys were potheads and their futures would be spent in the lower echelons of the retail trade, Mr. Bunting couldn't help but feel a small glimmer of pride in knowing that while the school's snooty-ass English, math and history teachers may have fallen short of improving the intellectual lives of Booby and Turk, their rope-climbing teacher had not failed them. That was what teaching was all about, as far as Mr. Bunting was concerned.

Finally, it was Eggerton's turn. Eggerton knew it would be foolish to try the pike climb or even the feet-dangling-from-below climb. Instead, he went directly for lock-and-lift.

Alas, he couldn't even hoist himself four feet off the mat. A very taciturn Mr. Bunting made a mark of failure next to Eggerton's name, and turned his attention to the next lock-and-lifter, satisfied, apparently, that the skinny underachiever named Eggerton would never rise to the great heights in life ensured by a successful lock-and-lift ascension.

And then, for reasons that had nothing to do with Eggerton's failure at the rope—indeed, Mr. Bunting had put Eggerton's sorry episode completely out of mind by now—Mr. Bunting suddenly grew wistful, and remembered what it was like to be a pro football player, and how you could get laid in any city in the league simply by walking into a bar the night before the game and cocking your itsy-bitsy pinky finger at any little bird who happened to come cooing your way. Playing pro football definitely was better than teaching lock-and-lift to potheads like Booby and Turk.

"*Shit,*" *Mr. Bunting sighed in a whisper audible to his ears, only.* "*Life sucks.*"

And, so now, having never successfully achieved the act of rappelling in his life, Eggerton was faced with the very real task of hoisting himself off the sill of a window, over a protruding gutter, and onto the slippery black slate of the roof of his house. And there would be no mat nor brooding gym teacher below; indeed, all that separated Eggerton from the hard flagstone path across his front lawn was the thin midsummer afternoon air—molecules of oxygen and hydrogen and nitrogen gently floating in space, parting whenever Eggerton's body cleaved through them, nudging one another aside to make room, none offering what anyone could reasonably call sponginess, should the need arise.

Eggerton thought briefly about looking down but decided there would be no reason. No, his world no longer had anything to do with flagstone paths or grassy front yards, or ex-Navy lawn-care specialists named Crowe who were very good at mowing grass in neat, parallel rows.

Eggerton leaned forward toward the gutter and quickly released his grip, then placed his hands, elbows bent and palms down, on the black slate. That done, he tested the slate—it was solid; Eggerton believed it would easily support his weight.

Eggerton drew in a deep breath, expanding his chest. He pressed down hard on the slate and commenced straightening his elbows.

All his muscled tensed, particularly those in his forehead, which seemed to be bearing the brunt of the act. The cords in his neck also tensed, and he felt his face form into a frozen, grotesque smile as he exerted even more pressure on his muscles.

He felt his weight leaving the windowsill. His toes were now off the sill. One inch. Two inches. Three inches.

Could he go on?

Eggerton realized he was about to fail. He was no more able to hoist himself up by the strength in his arms and arms alone than he was in high school, when he failed at lock-and-lift.

And so, this is where it would all end? Back on the windowsill of the secret attic room? After all this time, all the thought he had put into it, all the planning, all the personal sacrifice he made, to have it over and done with at virtually the same place he started?

Or, perhaps, he would just say "Screw it" to the windowsill and the secret attic room and merely let himself fall backward. It is likely the

My Life With Wings

fall would kill him, that he would snap his spine on the flagstone path or perhaps crush his skull; or, if he did live, it would be as an invalid, unable to use his arms and legs or control his bodily functions, pissing and shitting into bags for the rest of his life, growing old in a wheelchair, watching TV in the secret attic room, frozen in space, while time and the world just flew by outside.

Just flew right by...

Fuck that shit, Eggerton thought.

He pressed down hard on the slate. His toes lifted up another inch or two; his naval was now level with the gutter.

Eggerton tensed the muscles in his back. Suddenly, he felt a gust of cool wind, and then, quite unexpectedly, his hips hoisted themselves over the gutter. He was shocked at how effortlessly he had done that. And yet, this was no time to think things through.

He planted a knee firmly on the slate, steadied himself with his hands and shook his head to clear his thoughts.

And then, Eggerton stood on the black slate roof of the house he had bought eons and eons ago, before he grew wings.

Chapter Thirty

Junie planned to lead Simon, George and Donny into a private room with Martin and Mouse. Martin would then give them the background of Eggerton's story, explain the book and answer their questions. She planned to keep their attention for a half-hour or so, giving them more opportunities to consume alcohol. When she felt they were ready to get serious about bidding for the rights and also, when each executive was liquored up a bit, she would dispatch Mouse to retrieve Eggerton.

Once Eggerton entered the room, they could look him over and decide for themselves whether they would want anything to do with the project. Junie hoped all three would want in. If one or two rose to leave, that would be fine; there would still be a sale. But she needed two to auction the book; three would be better.

Junie intended to kick Martin out of the room when the actual bidding commenced. She wasn't at all sure he would even be in the final plans.

She hoped it wouldn't happen; she was fond of Martin and appreciated the work he had put in so far on *My Life With Wings*, but business was business: If the publisher wanted him out, there would be nothing she could do about it. After all, he could represent an unncessary expense. A co-author would, of course, receive a share of the profits. And if the film rights were sold, well, Martin would receive a share of those profits as well. Martin told Junie that Eggerton was his former co-worker at a newspaper. Surely, Junie thought, Eggerton must have some writing talent of his own. Can't he tell his own story? Would he really need a co-author?

And besides, Martin still had to finish the Piss Book. Junie called BBS the Piss Book behind Martin's back. Sometimes, she even just thought of it in terms of the PB. Whenever the notion of the PB passed through her brain she couldn't help but giggle. She thought the PB was a fairly ridiculous effort at literature and that it would hardly sell. No, MLWW was a much better gamble.

Junie thought more about the upcoming auction with the publishing executives. She didn't know yet whether to kick Mouse out of the room. Mouse obviously had the brains of a doorknob; yet, Junie couldn't help but notice how much time Simon was spending staring at Mouse's breasts. She decided to play it by ear; if Simon seemed to have the most interest in the book, she would permit Mouse to stay in the room. If the bidding got hot and heavy, perhaps she could induce Mouse to bend over so Simon could look down her top. She did the math and calculated that every time Simon stared at Mouse's chest his bid would rise by 5 percent. Maybe even 10 percent. She had been to auctions with Simon before and knew very well how to gauge his interest in a book.

Deep down, though, Junie didn't trust Mouse. After all, Martin told her that Mouse and Eggerton were divorced and yet, after Eggerton found himself sporting wings Mouse learned of this development in his life and moved back in with him. She suspected Mouse's motives were driven entirely by the opportunity to cash in on her ex-husband's wings. Even so, Junie thought that Mouse could find a way to really fuck up the auction.

Soon after entering the party Junie sized up Mouse and concluded it would be in everyone's interest if she kept a tight rein on her. And so, she grabbed Mouse's hand, held on tight and resolved not to let go until the auction commenced.

My Life With Wings

She wasn't sure what to do with Eggerton. On one hand, she thought his presence might be distracting as he sat there, wings akimbo, while she tried to hash out a serious literary contract. On the other hand, she thought having him sit there might give her the psychological advantage: He would be paraded in front of them, so to speak, as the prize they would have to snatch.

Junie Glaucous mulled all this over while the party crowded around her. She tugged on Mouse's hand, pulling the startled hostess toward her. She turned her head at the very last second, so that her lips met Mouse's ear.

"Isn't this a wonderful party?" she said.

Chapter Thirty-one

Mouse felt the tug of the awful woman's hand and feared her arm was about to be pulled out of its socket.

"Isn't this a wonderful party?" Junie said, a smile crossing her face ear to ear.

Mouse nearly vomited at the odor of the woman's breath. It smelled of cheap wine and stale cigarettes.

"Yes. . .I guess. . ." Mouse answered.

By now, Mouse was suffering through a painful headache. A super migraine; pounding sledgehammers, locomotives racing, anvils clanging on the concrete, fingernails scraping across the slate board, and so on. Her need to urinate had grown even more acute. She found herself pressing her knees together, hoping that would help shrink her bladder to an acceptable size. It did not.

Mouse felt a chill.

"Are you OK?"

She looked up. It was Crane. He was with Woody.

"I have a headache," she said.

"Let The Cranester take care of that," said Crane, grateful that he could assist, medically. "Do you have aspirin in the house?"

"I don't know, maybe in the bathroom."

"You should take some," said Crane, delighted with himself for prescribing a treatment within the boundaries of acceptable medical procedure.

He smiled at her. "Is there more beer inside?" he asked.

"Yes, I'm sure there is."

"Let's go," he said to Woody, "I'm thirsty."

"Me, too," said Woody.

The two men headed inside. As he walked away, Crane turned his head over his shoulder and winked impishly at Mouse.

Mouse wondered how Eggerton was doing. She knew she should check on him. She was about to tell Junie that she really had to find Eggerton, and wouldn't she be a dear and release her hand, when two men approached her. She didn't recognize them.

"Nice party," said one man.

"Yeah," said the other man.

One man was about 45 or 50; the other, much younger. Perhaps 20 or 25. The older man was completely bald although he sported a Van Dyke beard. He wore a gold earring in one ear, green fatigue Army-style pants and a pair of high black leather boots. He wore a T-shirt that said "Clyde's Army-Navy Surplus Store." The younger man was tall and thin and dressed similarly, only his T-shirt said, "Mötley Crüe." He also seemed to have a problem with acne.

The older man identified himself as Clyde, quickly adding that he is owner of Clyde's Army-Navy Surplus Store. He said Woody invited them to the party. He said he didn't know Woody terribly well, but Woody had been in the store recently to buy an Army cot and told him about this guy who lived nearby who actually grew a set of wings.

And then, just the other day, Clyde stopped into the Happy Buffalo Wing for some buffalo wings (he enjoyed extra spicy sauce) when, quite coincidentally, he met up again with Woody, who appeared to be the manager of the local Happy Buffalo Wing emporium, and Woody said to him, "Remember that guy with wings? Well, he's having a party. I'm sure he wouldn't mind meeting you." And Clyde said to himself, "Well, what the fuck, I ain't exactly doing anything, so why the shit not?"

Clyde said the kid works in the store. Clyde hoped Mouse wouldn't mind that he brought the kid along. He said the kid doesn't get out much. He said the kid spends most of his time reading comic books.

Clyde said he doesn't think the kid should spend so much time reading comic books.

Mouse said she didn't mind. Clyde said he was glad to hear that.

As Clyde finished his story, Mouse noticed two women standing nearby. Each woman held a glass of wine. One woman was tall and thin; she wore rimless granny glasses, a long cotton skirt and sandals. She wore a tight T-shirt sporting a picture of Dumbo the elephant. A mouse dressed in a red ringmaster's costume sat perched in Dumbo's hat.

She extended a hand to Mouse. "My name is Kiwi; I'm a friend of Eggerton's."

Mouse shook Kiwi's hand with her free hand. She hoped Kiwi would let her hand go. How terrible, she thought, to be chained to two women, hand to hand.

Mouse was immensely grateful when Kiwi let go of her hand very quickly. She wanted to kiss Kiwi for the gesture.

"My name is Lazuli," said the other woman. "I'm a friend, too."

"Hello," said Mouse.

Lazuli did not extend her hand to Mouse. That was fine with Mouse. She didn't know Lazuli; indeed, Lazuli could be another hand-shaker.

Lazuli was not quite as tall as Kiwi, but she was rail-thin. She wore tight jeans, a red tube top and very dark sunglasses. Mouse stared hard, but was unable to see Lazuli's eyes through her glasses.

"That's my real name; I'm not making it up."

Mouse smiled. "I'm sure it is," she said.

Clyde laughed.

"You girls like pup tents?" he asked.

"Do we ever!" announced Kiwi.

"Do you want to see mine?" asked Clyde.

He smiled devilishly.

"Do we ever!" said Kiwi.

Clyde, Kiwi, Lazuli and the kid who likes comic books then backed away from Mouse, presumably to make plans to see Clyde's pup tent.

Chapter Thirty-two

Eggerton stepped carefully higher on the slate roof, finally coming to a stop with his feet straddling the peak of the roof. He noticed the roof, sitting exposed to the sun, was uncomfortably hot. He broke into a heavy sweat.

He sat down, resting his rump on the peak. Below, he heard voices. He could see the party guests, milling around on the terra cotta patio, enjoying themselves. For reasons he couldn't explain, their enjoyment made him feel good. He supposed he should join them, but was in no hurry.

Chapter Thirty-three

"When can we see the guest of honor?" asked George.

Donny spoke up as well. "Yes, he said, "when can we see the guest of honor, this fellow with wings?"

"Oh...soon," said Junie.

She turned to Mouse and was about to instruct her to lead them to a quiet corner of the house for their meeting with Eggerton when a man approached Martin.

Martin's eyes lit up. "You came!" he smiled.

"Wouldn't miss this, buddy," said the man.

"This is Griffin, everybody."

Martin was met with some puzzled looks.

"Griffin, the true star of the BBS book," Martin said.

Martin shoved his hands into his pockets. He looked from side to side to check the expressions on everybody's faces. Again, though, he found his words were met with furrowed brows.

"Everybody, this is Griffin," Martin said again, evidently unaware that he had just, not more than five seconds earlier, already introduced the man whose urinary tract would soon be described in detail over the course of 50,000 words.

Griffin gave everyone an "Aww, shucks" mock smile, as if to say the notoriety he expected to soon receive as the focal point of a milestone in literature was quite undeserved.

Griffin was about average size; he had very curly red hair and burnt orange freckles across his face. He wore cut-off blue jeans and a white undershirt—the type without sleeves. Red freckles were splayed across his shoulders and upper back. He appeared also to have a habit of running his fingers through his hair as he spoke, which exposed his curly red underarm hair. Mouse was mildly appalled.

"Hey, it's like this," said Griffin, fingering his hair and exposing his hairy underarms, "if a lot of people read my buddy's book, and they realize they have this piss-in-public phobia, like I do, then maybe some good will come of it, after all."

Donny laughed out loud.

"I'll be so anxious to read Martin's book," he said. Of course, Donny had no intention to read Martin's book. He had no interest in Bashful Bladder Syndrome and suspected few other people would as well.

"Do you want a beer?" asked Mouse.

"Sure, as long as there's a lock on the bathroom door," said Griffin.

Mouse was about to tell Junie that she would have to let go of her hand so she could find a beer for Griffin, when Junie tugged again on her hand, drawing her close to her body. Mouse winced with pain, again. Junie leaned over toward Mouse. She said, "Mary Anne, dear, can you find us. . ."

She was interrupted by these words: "Fuck off asshole!"

Mouse turned her head toward the sound. Hendrix, that strange fellow who arrived with Crane, shouted the warning to Evan, the tall man with the pinking shears-cut Event Staff T-shirt who walked in with Woody.

"No, you fuck off!" Evan answered back.

Then, Hendrix shoved Evan. Hendrix was a strong man, well-muscled, an athlete, a linebacker. His shove knocked Evan to the hard terra cotta patio. Evan fell hard, hitting his head on the tiles.

My Life With Wings

"Oh, my!" said Mouse.

"A fight!" said Simon. He had taken his eyes off Mouse's breasts for the first time in several minutes. Anybody who knew Simon knew very well that if anything could divert his attention from a woman's breasts it was a good fight between two sweaty, enraged, drunk, stupid men.

Mouse wanted to rush over to the scuffle, but Junie continued holding her prisoner. The excitement of the moment prompted Junie to clench Mouse's hand even harder. Mouse glanced at Junie. She was clearly enraged.

"Get away from him!" Junie screamed. Her shriek sounded unwordly to Mouse, the tone screeching from Junie's lungs pierced Mouse's eardrums like a knife slicing through cheese. Junie was, of course, fearful that this fight could somehow ruin the auction—that the fisticuffs would drive Simon, George and Donny out of the house. She desperately wanted these two rambunctious assholes to take their dispute somewhere else.

But that wasn't about to happen. Hendrix aimed to finish the fight the only way he knew how, and that was to beat the crap out of Evan.

And so, Hendrix jumped onto Evan and started punching him in the stomach. Evan screamed in pain. Hendrix straddled Evan's chest. He brought his fist back, ready to punch Evan in the face.

High above, on the roof, Eggerton saw the fight break out. He didn't know why Hendrix suddenly resorted to violence; lord knows, he hadn't liked the creepy guy since Crane brought him around to the secret attic room several weeks ago.

But he did see the shove and he did see the tall man fall back onto the terra cotta tiles, and he did see Hendrix take advantage of the fallen fellow by kneeling over him. And he did hear that obnoxious woman standing next to Mouse let out a scream that seemed to strip the leaves off of all the nearby trees.

Eggerton left the roof. He did it quite unconsciously, as though human flight was the most natural of acts. His wings propelled him airborne; he swooped over the patio, and then fluttered his wings so he could hang suspended over the action.

"Hey, you!" he shouted from above in a squeaky chirp. "Don't hit that man!"

Everyone on the patio stood frozen. Hendrix, his arm raised and about to be used for punching the fallen man, turned to look above. He was immediately blinded by the glare, as was Evan, who was also straining to see what was going on.

"Look at dat der!" said the comic book reader who had come with Clyde.

"Oh!" said Kiwi.

"It's true!" said George.

"Shit me!" shouted Duckie.

And then, in a much milder tone, she repeated the words. "Shit me," she said.

No one noticed until a short time later, but the sight of Eggerton flapping his wings over the terra cotta patio was fatal to old Dr. Hitchcock. He was so startled at seeing Eggerton hovering in mid-air that his heart seized on him. He was dead before his forehead dropped onto the glass-topped Cinzano table.

Back on the terra cotta patio, Junie Glaucous said, "Oh! Mr. Eggerton, come down please."

Crane and Woody dashed out of the house.

"What the fuck?" said Woody.

Eggerton allowed himself to drop a few feet lower. He pointed at Hendrix. "Get off him," he said.

Hendrix let his arm drop. He stood and backed away from Evan. Woody rushed to Evan and helped him to his feet. Evan was pale and woozy. His head was bleeding.

Mouse noticed Junie's grip was tighter now than ever. At that moment, she had enough of Junie-Fucking-Glaucous.

"Junie!" she shouted.

No answer. Junie's attention was transfixed on the man floating above her in the air.

"Junie!" Mouse said a second time, even louder now.

Still, no answer.

Mouse whipped Junie's arm, forcing the woman to turn awkwardly toward her. Mouse reared back with her free hand and let a punch fly. She caught Junie in the jaw; the literary agent fell hard onto the terra cotta patio, letting go of Mouse's hand as she fell. Later, Junie would

My Life With Wings

discover the blow loosened three teeth. She declined to sue after consulting a lawyer who told her she had no case.

Now, free of Junie's grip, Mouse ran to the center of the terra cotta patio.

"Hey!" Mouse shouted toward her ex-husband.

"Hey!" said Eggerton.

Chapter Thirty-four

For weeks, Martin and Junie pursued Eggerton relentlessly but he steadfastly refused to sign a publishing contract. They each made many visits to Eggerton's house. Finally, they gave up. That was fine with Mouse. She wanted nothing more to do with Junie Glaucous.

Oddly, the only book anyone who attended the party that day would write was authored by Hendrix, of all people. Later that summer, Hendrix returned to his college football team. He had such a good season that he was drafted by the Arizona Cardinals in the NFL. He was a low draft pick, to be sure, but he turned out to be a budding star. Hendrix went on to have a successful career with the Cardinals, making three trips to the Pro Bowl.

Along the way he found many earning opportunities. In addition to signing a series of hefty contracts with the Cardinals, he became something of a local celebrity in the greater Phoenix area. He appeared in local TV commercials, helping car dealers sell their vehicles. He cut ribbons to open supermarkets. He signed autographs at convenience stores all over Arizona. He appeared on local sports radio talk shows, airing his well-received but in truth rather vapid opinions on the state of sports in the state of Arizona.

He remained very busy because, in truth, he had never managed his money well, squandering his savings on a series of bad investments. For example, he invested $1 million in an app that placed an image of the head of the app owner onto the body of a pro football player. Once engaging the app, the owner could watch himself or herself participate in an NFL play. The app owner could play quarterback and make a pass or play wide receiver and catch the pass or play defensive back and intercept the pass. Or sack the quarterback. Or kick a field goal. Or return a punt for a touchdown. Or whatever.

While the app proved to be very popular it was not profitable. The app developers had to pay royalties to all the players whose bodies were co-opted for the performances. And that proved to be a very hefty price. All the players who gave permission for their bodies to be used in the app were superstars and they all had agents who demanded a lot of money for their clients. Eventually, the startup that developed the app went bankrupt and all investors lost their money. In fact, though, Hendrix was the lone investor.

A similar series of financial pratfalls seemed to plague Hendrix for his entire career in professional football and so, when he finally retired from the game, he was virtually penniless. But he was soon contacted by a sports biography publisher who offered him $250,000 for his story. Hendrix gladly accepted the deal and spent three weeks dictating his life's story to a newspaper sportswriter retained by the publisher to ghost-write the book.

It was during the course of his interview with the sportswriter that Hendrix related the anecdote about the man with wings swooping down on him while he held Evan at bay on the terra cotta patio. The sportswriter hardly believed the story, but kept his mouth shut and let his digital voice recorder run.

The book, titled, *Flying Linebacker*, make quite a splash. Hendrix and the sportswriter filled most of *Flying Linebacker* with tales of drug

My Life With Wings

use and drunken debauchery. There were so many lurid tales related in the book involving sex, drugs and booze that none of the critics who reviewed *Flying Linebacker* paid much attention to the single sentence in the book relating the story about the man with wings. Here is that sentence:

> *One time, I was at a party and was so drunk and stoned I swear this guy with wings came flying down at me.*

Chapter Thirty-five

Mouse continued to live in Eggerton's house, although she rarely saw her ex-husband. He instructed her to leave the window of the secret attic room open so that he might come and go at will.

He continued to sleep on the Army cot in the secret attic room when he was home, which was not too often. Indeed, he would sometimes fly away for six weeks or more.

During one of his extended absences, Mouse made her way to the secret attic room and found the manila folder under the cot.

She read through his notes several times. She found the stories about the elephant and the mouse, the rudimentary flying machine and the other dreams. She also found the cash register receipt from Clyde's Army-Navy Surplus Store. On the back of the receipt was written these words: "Lock-and-lift." Mouse gave those words a lot of thought but ultimately could not imagine what they could mean.

Mouse developed a habit of going for long walks. Often, she would walk for several miles. She took long walks because she wanted to think about Eggerton, and where he might have gone. Whenever he was home she would ask where he spent most of his time these days, but he refused to answer.

Finally, she stopped asking.

One day, at the end of a long walk, she found herself at the steps of the public library. It was an old building, constructed of stone and masonry in the Greco-Roman style of architecture. In front of the library, holding up an elaborate stone arch, were six tall columns.

She ascended the stone steps in front of the library, then sat down on a plinth. She was alone. Nobody else was sitting on any of the nearby plinths.

The plinth was hard and hurt her ass. It was also cold.

Mouse felt a chill.

She wished for wings.

My Life With Wings

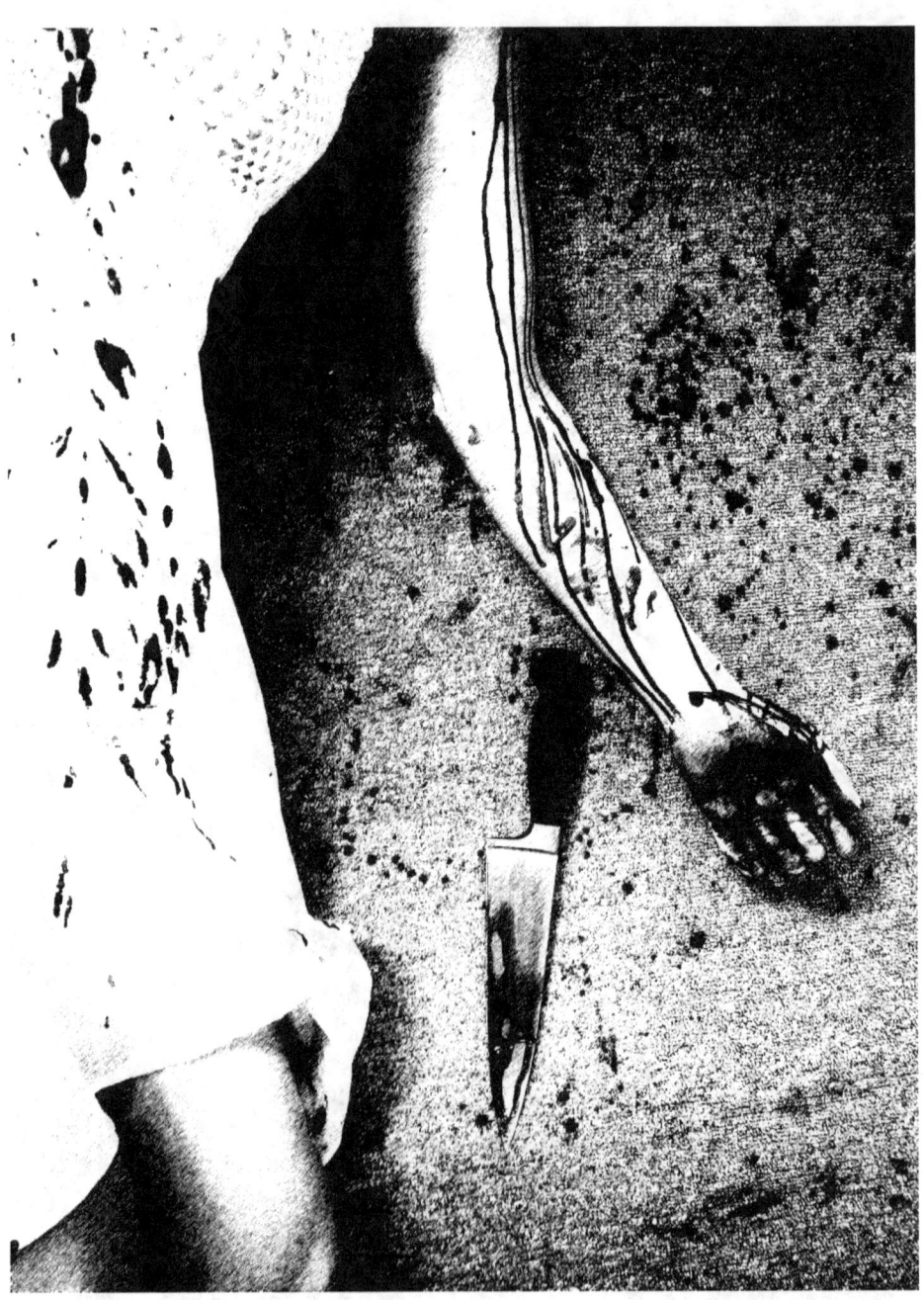

Adult Situations, Profanity, Nudity, Sex, Violence

Paul eased the old Chevy into his driveway, being careful not to arouse attention in the neighborhood. After all, his dad had already told him he'd take away the keys again if he caught him laying wheels or fishtailing or turfing anybody's lawn.

He killed the ignition, then sat listening to the funky beat of the demo track that his band cut earlier that evening. When the track ended he smiled and took one final slurp from the beer can that had been cradled in his lap on the ride home.

He tossed the empty can under the seat; it made a soft aluminum clank against the dozen or so other beer cans that Paul shoved there over the past several nights. Got to clean out the car, he thought. Paul wiped the stale foam away from his lips, stubbed out his Marlboro, popped a mint into his mouth on the rare chance his mom or dad was still up and went into the house.

Paul played bass in a band with three friends from high school. Eddie was the drummer. Phil played lead guitar. Cindy did the vocals. She also tapped a tambourine against her hip but Paul found that when it came to the art of the tambourine, Cindy still had a lot to learn.

No matter. Cindy was really hot. She always wore really tight jeans or really short skirts. Her hair was long and silky, hanging almost to her ass. Paul and Cindy had started dating a couple of weeks ago.

It was just before 4 a.m. and he was punk sore. After cutting the track in Joe's basement, Paul and Cindy grabbed some pizza and then wrestled in the back seat of the Chevy for a few short minutes. It was their third date and she still wasn't giving him anything more than bare tit. Cripes, Paul thought, would be love to get into her pants.

Paul kept a foil-wrapped condom in his wallet. It had been there for nearly two years and made a definitive "O" impression in the soft leather of his wallet. He loved to casually take out his wallet in front of his friends so he could show off the O.

He looked on the O in his wallet as a badge of honor—a show of maturity and machismo. Only the coolest dudes kept condoms in their wallets and only the coolest dudes had the telltale O's. Paul had the condom and he had the O and only Paul and Paul alone knew the awful truth that he had never come close to using it.

And only Paul knew the further truth about the condom—that he had lifted it from his dad's bureau drawer. Paul was scared shitless of the day when he would have to walk into a pharmacy and buy a pack of condoms.

Paul was careful not to make noise as he entered the house. He also didn't have to turn on the lights to find his way. Paul's mother hadn't rearranged the furniture since Bush was in the White House. Paul walked knowingly through the familiar darkness, as a blind man would.

Paul didn't think he was a bit tired. He walked into the kitchen and thought briefly about a snack but decided he wasn't hungry. He did grab himself one of his dad's Buds, though, and made a mental note to throw away the can this time. Last time, cripes, he had left it on the kitchen table and his dad had shit purple the next morning. Cripes.

He popped open the beer then went back into the living room where he picked up the TV remote, turned on the set and selected the on-screen menu.

He flopped down on the sofa and scrolled through the menu until his eye caught the synopsis of a film about to begin on a cable channel that called itself the Night Owl Network. The description of the movie read:

Adult Situations, Profanity, Nudity, Sex, Violence

Camp Blood. One Star. (R) Debi Tucker. Kim Rogers, Steve Turner. A homicidal maniac chops up randy teens at a summer camp. Adult situations, profanity, nudity, sex, violence. 112 minutes.

Just what he needed to get his mind off Cindy: a good slasher flick! Cindy didn't like to go to those kind of movies. In his three dates with her they had seen three gooey chick-flicks with a lot of gawd-awful acting about upwardly mobile snobs having babies and screwing up their relationships. No homicides, no blood, no cops, no AK47s blasting up the screen. OK, there was some occasional nudity in those chick-flicks, which was good, but for the most part Paul found the movies boring. Cindy always sat there transfixed, invariably shoving his hand off her boob.

And so as the movie rolled on Paul would be hard-pressed to stay awake. Cindy liked to talk about the movie afterward and Paul often found himself at a loss to discuss the film—even though he had just seen it (more or less). He usually just agreed with everything Cindy said, which seemed to make her happy.

One time he did suggest they take in something with a bit more action. It was a police drama that earned high ratings on Rotten Tomatoes. Cindy sniffed that it had too much violence and too much profanity and too much sex and she had no interest in it at all. Paul could only admit to himself that he was not shocked by her taste.

So Paul found himself going to movies with four stars that Cindy told him the critics were crazy about. Paul shrugged, kept his mouth shut and went along. Just about the only thing that kept him going through the flicks was a steady supply of buttered popcorn and the thought of getting Cindy into the backseat of the Chevy after the film and getting her pants down around her knees. Of course, that hadn't happened yet and if you had asked Paul at this particular moment about the likelihood of it ever happening he would tell you, for cripes sake, that it probably would never happen. At least not to him.

And why not? Cripes, Paul thought, all his friends seemed to be getting laid. Or, at least, they said they were. Paul wondered about that a lot. Every Monday morning Eddie and Phil would regale him with tales of their weekend conquests. Paul would respond in kind and everybody seemed to be buying the act. If he thought Eddie or Phil were doubting him Paul had merely to find an excuse to reach into his wallet. which would give him the opportunity to show off his condom and the wonderful O the rolled up ring of latex made in the leather.

But Paul had been doubting the stories Eddie and Phil told him ever since he started dating Cindy. Eddie had also dated Cindy but they broke up after a few weeks. When Paul started taking her out Eddie assured him that Cindy would deliver the goods. Of course, she hadn't. Paul had his doubts about Phil, too. Paul started noticing an O in Phil's wallet, which Paul knew all too well was no sign of coital success.

It was all very frustrating, this sex business.

Still a virgin at 18. Paul flopped down on the sofa, punched the remote control and waited to be entertained.

Camp Blood started off with some creepy psycho music rolling over the credits while pubescent girls shrieked and screamed in the background. Cripes, thought Paul, no wonder this flick got one star. He sipped his beer. Maybe, he thought, he should just go to bed after all.

Pretty soon he nodded off, dozing in front of the TV while the Bud dangled from his fingers. He shook himself awake when somebody screamed on the screen; then he noticed the precarious position of the beer. Cripes, he thought, all I have to do is spill the goddamned beer on the goddamned carpet and mom will shit purple. He put the beer on the end table next to the sofa and was asleep again within seconds.

"Paul…Paul, honey…wake up."

Paul shook himself out of his coma, struggling under the weight of his eyelids. They felt like they each weighed a ton. "Huh?" he managed to say.

"How's it going, dude?"

Paul looked around. Nobody else was in the room. Then he glanced at the TV screen through itchy eyes. There was a beautiful blonde babe looking back at him, smiling. She had blue eyes and gorgeous skin. Perfect teeth and naked shoulders. As if on cue, the camera panned back a bit, showing her upper torso. She wore a white tube top that did wonders for her boobs. She waved her hand again and jiggled.

Adult Situations, Profanity, Nudity, Sex, Violence

"It's Paul, right? That's your name, right?"

Paul wondered whether he was drunk. He picked up the Bud off the end table and swished it around. Clearly, there was half the beer left. Can you get drunk on half a beer? He took a swig. It was warm and flat. He swallowed. Finally, he said, "Who are you?"

"Debi Tucker, silly. I'm in the movie."

He nodded. "Yeah, I guess you are." He thought for a moment "You're a pretty good actress." It was the best line he could come up with. Honestly, he didn't know what kind of an actress she was because except for the opening credits he hadn't seen any of the movie.

"Hey, thanks." she said. "Would you like to come in here with me?"

Paul found her to be unusually bright and perky, given the fact that it was after 4 a.m. And for reasons Paul simply could not explain to himself, he found nothing unusual in the idea of jumping into the TV screen.

"How do I do that?"

"Just walk toward the TV. When you get really close to the screen. I'll reach out and pull you in. It's easy, you'll see."

Well, cripes, what the hell, Paul thought. He picked up his beer, carried it with him over to the screen and suddenly was shocked by a flash of blinding light. He gasped, then felt a hand on his arm and a yank and, just like that, he was standing in the countryside on a sunny warm day with Debi Tucker who, Paul immediately noticed, looked even better in her tube top now than when he first saw her on TV. She was also wearing cut-off jeans that showed off no small portion of her tight teen-aged ass. Cripes, Paul thought.

"I told you it would be easy," she said. "Come on, I'll show you around."

She took his hand and led him down a path to a shady grove where about a dozen kids his age were sitting around picnic tables. Tall oak trees towered overhead, providing a cool darkness over the grove. There was a case of beer by one of the tables. Suddenly, one of the boys looked up and waved.

"Hi Debi...Hi Paul," he said. "Hey, Paul, throw away that stale old Bud and have a fresh one. He reached into the case and took out a can, then tossed it to Paul. It was icy to the touch. Paul flipped off the top and was sprayed with some cool froth. All the kids around the picnic tables laughed. Paul laughed, too, and then he took a long cold slurp from the brew. He also threw away the old Bud can. Cripes, Paul thought to himself, his dad will never find the can here.

He laughed again. This was great, being in the movies.

The boy who tossed the can of beer to Paul came running over. He stuck out his hand.

"I'm Steve," he said.

Paul shook his hand. Steve was tall, tanned and athletic. He wore a polo shirt, cut-off jeans and sandals. Steve told Paul there was plenty to do—tennis and basketball if he cared for sports or even swimming. The camp has a terrific lake, he said.

Steve turned to Debi. He said, "Kim wants to go over the plans for the barbecue tonight. She wants to know whether hot dogs and hamburgers are OK or whether we should try something more exotic." Debi nodded and jogged down to the picnic tables, where some girls were sitting.

Paul found himself alone with Steve. "Debi is a great chick," Steve said. Paul agreed. "We used to date," Steve continued. "You'll enjoy your time together."

Paul nodded. He was going to tell Steve how Debi was able to pull him into the TV but then Steve started talking again. "She's a great piece of ass, too," he said.

"Huh?"

Steve smiled, showing perfect white teeth. "I should know," he said. "Man, did I love getting my hands on her boobs."

Paul arched his eyebrows. He suddenly thought of Cindy and the O in his wallet. Cindy let him touch her boobs and that's all she let him touch. Paul wanted to ask Steve if Debi went further than that but he suddenly felt very unsure of himself.

He felt, well, like a virgin.

Paul looked at Steve.

"Does she..."

Steve nodded. "Like a fish."

Just then Debi returned. She told Steve the plans for the barbecue were set. Steve said he was looking forward to it; he waved to Debi and Paul and trotted back to the picnic tables. Steve, Paul concluded, was no Eddie. This time Paul believed.

Adult Situations, Profanity, Nudity, Sex, Violence

Debi and Paul walked on. They passed some tennis courts where some teens were playing, then some basketball courts where a pick-up game was in progress. Occasionally, they would meet some young people on the path and Debi stopped to chat with them for a bit, always introducing Paul—who never had much to say. It was incredible, though. All the babes were great looking, just like they always were in the movies. All the boys were matinee-idol handsome, just like they always were in the movies. Paul wondered why none of them had zits.

Debi told Paul about her career, how she had been performing on stage since she was a little girl. She made a few TV commercials, had done some dinner theater and occasionally landed a movie role, although none of the films were critical successes and none were what you would call big-budget productions. Usually, she would end up as the victim of a homicidal maniac sometime midway through the first or second reel. Lately, the directors were insisting on nude scenes. Debi told him it didn't really bother her to do a nude scene, although she doubted how important they were to the plots. She giggled. Acting paid well, though, and she hoped to be landing some more significant roles soon.

Paul told Debi that he was nearly finished high school but he was unsure of what he planned to do with his future. He told Debi about the track he had just cut with his band mates and how he thought the band had some real promise, and wouldn't it be nice to land some gigs. He didn't tell Debi that he was dating the band's singer but he wasn't very happy because Cindy refused to go past second base. He found it easy to talk to Debi and wondered why he could never talk to Cindy that way.

Debi led on. Paul noticed the sun was setting and it was getting to be late in the afternoon. "Want to go swimming?" Debi asked. Paul said it sounded like a good idea. Debi led him to a lakeside. Steve had been right; the camp has a terrific lake. Its ripple-free glass surface stretched out in front of Paul and Debi making Paul wonder whether it would be OK to destroy the late-afternoon calm with a splash. He was caught up in the gentle sprawling vista before him when he felt Debi's touch. Her hand glided down his arm, sending shivers through him.

Debi took a step away from Paul, then turned to face him and pulled off her tube top, exposing firm round breasts that were accented by her tan lines. She threw back her bead, shaking her blonde hair, then parted her lips and hooked her thumbs into the waistband of her cutoffs. She slipped them off. She wasn't wearing underwear. Cripes, Paul thought.

"Come on in, silly," she laughed. She kicked sand at Paul, then turned and ran splashing into the lake.

With 18 years of pent-up virginity bursting for freedom; with absolutely no thought at all about that frigid bitch Cindy, with no regard whatsoever for his broken-down old Chevy and its pathetic aluminum block engine, with neither cares nor woes about his anal retentive parents, Paul tore off his T-shirt, kicked off his sneakers, wrestled his jeans to the ground and ran out of his jockey shorts. He splashed into the lake after Debi and never once felt the numbing cold attack the crack of his ass.

They made love on the beach. He briefly thought of asking Debi whether she wanted him to take the O out of his wallet, but that thought quickly evaporated as Debi wrapped her arms around his neck, pressing her lips into his. As their lovemaking was nearing an end Debi wrapped her legs around Paul's ass and shrieked. Paul was certain they both climaxed at the same time—which is pretty bitchin' for your first time out, for cripes sakes. Afterward, he shared a cigarette with Debi—just like they do in the movies.

Debi told Paul that it was getting dark and they had better be getting back. Paul dressed quickly, although he had no idea where they were going. After all, he had no intentions of going back to his living room. Eddie and Phil will just have to find a new bass player, Paul decided.

They walked back up the path from the lake. Paul let Debi lead, not really paying attention to the trail. The setting sun warmed the back of his neck, giving him a comfortable perspiration beneath his shirt. It was a totally different feeling than he had after spending an evening with Cindy. After the pizza and after the dopey four-star movie and after the unsatisfying groping in the back seat of the Chevy would finally come to an end, Paul would drive her home and deposit Cindy at her front door. There would be some small talk, then a kiss and a wave and a frustrating drive home.

He would sweat then, too, but that would be a cold, chilling sweat—a sweat that would make him thirsty and hanker for a cold beer that he could hold between his thighs for the drive home.

Adult Situations, Profanity, Nudity, Sex, Violence

But this was different. Paul wanted a beer, to be sure, but he wanted to share it with Debi and laugh with her and talk about the movies some more and maybe a little later she would take him down to the lake for a midnight swim and more sex in the sand. Paul shook himself out of his daydream. For now, he was satisfied simply to be walking hand-in-hand with this blonde-haired B-movie goddess. He squeezed her hand and found himself admiring the rustic landscape as they walked. He was caught up in the beauty of the bucolic terrain and was overwhelmed by the rays of the setting sun bursting through the treetops around them.

That's when Debi screamed.

Paul turned and immediately saw what had frightened her. It was the body of a girl, sprawled on the path before them. She was a dark-haired beauty, probably one of the kids he saw earlier in the day at the picnic grove. Her chest had been caved in, a wide and ugly gash leaching blood.

Debi was still wailing away. Cripes, Paul thought, if she would shut up be could think this out. He grabbed Debi, pulled her around the body and led her running up the path. Paul was surprised at how cool he was. When they reached a clearing, they stopped.

"Who was she?"

Debi's complexion had turned white. Paul saw that she was shivering, that her lips had turned blue.

Paul thought she might be in shock. Just then, she dropped to her knees and started sobbing.

"Debi…please, talk to me. Who was she?"

Paul dropped to his knees. too, and started shaking her shoulders. Maybe he should slap her in the face. Isn't that what they do in the movies?

He tried it. Paul used the back of his hand and gave her a sharp and distinct smack across her teeth. He didn't want to hurt Debi, just startle her enough so he could get a coherent answer out of her. It worked. She looked at him with runny red eyes, breathing heavily while trying to sniff back the tears.

"Debi, who was she?"

"It was Kim," Debi said. "Kim Rogers, one of the girls from the movie. We had our screen test together"

"Do you have any idea who killed her?"

Debi looked down at the ground and shook her head.

"We've got to find shelter and call the police," Paul said. He reached into his pocket and took out his phone. No signal. Of course, he thought, why would I expect cellular bars inside my TV?

He turned to Debi. "Do you know where we can find a land line?"

Debi nodded. She told him there was a telephone at the camp office, which was just beyond the picnic grove they had visited earlier that day. They walked briskly up the path. Neither wanted to talk.

Before long they came upon the bodies of two more teens. One boy, one girl. Paul thought the boy was Steve. His arm had been hacked off and his throat was slashed. The girl had a deep knife wound in her back.

Debi was hysterical. She put her hands to her head and screamed—a loud, piercing scream that shattered Paul's eardrums and made him wish he was back behind the wheel of the Chevy. Cripes, Paul thought, Cindy never let him get into her pants but at least she never screamed, either.

Paul collapsed to his knees and buried his face in his hands; he felt like throwing up, but he suppressed the urge. No, Paul said to himself, this can't be happening, this just can't be happening. The day had been going so well—it wasn't fair that it had to be ruined this way.

He dropped his hands and saw the two bodies again. He had only chatted with Steve briefly but found him to be a friendly enough dude. After all, he urged Paul to go for it with Debi. "Like a fish," Steve told him. Paul wasn't sure how fish practice coitus, but he had a deep suspicion that Steve didn't feel the need to show off an O in his wallet. Paul wondered whether Steve had been making it with the girl at his side when the killer came upon them. Then, Debi screamed again and that shocked Paul back to his senses. He grabbed Debi's hand and continued running up the path. The girl said nothing; he thought she might be in shock.

They passed the basketball court. The pick-up game had been interrupted by the killer: all the players were dead, some were dismembered. They passed the tennis court; more carnage. At the picnic grove some of the kids had been decapitated; others were impaled on fence posts.

Paul walked through it all, trying hard not to look at the carnage that seemed to be everywhere. Paul thought about the living room at home

Adult Situations, Profanity, Nudity, Sex, Violence

and suddenly remembered he hadn't turned off the TV before, well, before Debi invited him in. He wondered whether his mother and father were up now and watching this whole incredible story on the Night Owl Network. He thought about shouting out to them for help, but decided it would be silly.

The office was where Debi said it was. It was in a cabin which was, of course, locked. Paul led Debi around the back, found a trash can and heaved it through a window, shattering the glass. He climbed inside, then helped Debi in through the window.

There was a Coke machine against a wall—it was the type that dispensed the old-fashioned glass bottles. There was even a picture of a girl in a sailor suit painted on the door of the machine. The girl wore her sailor's cap at a jaunty angle. She winked and smiled broadly through blonde curls as she held up a bottle of Coca-Cola. Paul thought she looked like one of those child movie stars from the 1930s. Who, though? Shirley Temple, that's who. It had to be Shirley Temple because Paul simply didn't know any other child stars from the 1930s.

Paul regarded Debi. She was sobbing quietly. Her eyes were puffy from crying. He wanted to tell her that they would get out of this and that the police would find the killer.

And then what would they do? Paul thought briefly about taking her home with him, back to his living room. He put the thought out of his mind. Maybe they could find another camp—with a tennis court and a picnic grove and a beautiful, ripple-free lake where they could screw on the beach.

"Want a soda?" he asked.

Debi turned slowly and looked at him. She didn't answer, just sobbed some more. Paul looked at Shirley Temple. Shirley wanted a dollar for a Coke. He dug into his pocket. No cash.

Ever since they left the lake, Paul concluded, nothing had been going right.

He saw the phone on a desk. He crossed the room and picked up the receiver. No dial tone, just silence. Somehow, Paul knew the phone would be out. Cripes, he thought.

By now it was dark. Paul decided they would have to find a road, maybe flag down a driver and get help that way. But it would have to wait until tomorrow. No way did Paul want to stumble around the camp now. There was no telling whether the killer was still on the grounds, no telling where he may be lurking out there. Debi wasn't going to be much help, either. He was certain that he would have to find their way to the road because it was clear that Debi was just out of it.

His first inclination was to spend the night in the office but then Paul saw the broken window and knew that would be out of the question. There was no way to lock out the killer. Paul took Debi by the arm. "Come on," he said, "we've got to find a safe place to spend the night."

Paul eased Debi through the window again, then followed her out. They crept through the darkness, taking it one step at a time. Debi clutched hard against him and Paul could feel the naked feral fear ooze out of her. He wanted to comfort her, wanted somehow to reassure her. Paul said nothing. He was being honest with her: he knew he couldn't reassure her. And then Paul saw a barn up ahead. "We'll hide there," he said.

Paul didn't know much about barns but once inside he spotted the hay loft. He found an old wooden ladder and helped Debi scamper up; then he climbed up himself. The hay was refreshingly cool. It itched a little, but Paul thought he could get used to it although he doubted whether he would sleep that night. In fact, Paul decided it would be best not to sleep. He looked at Debi—she had balled herself into an almost fetal position. Paul wondered whether she was asleep but decided not to ask her. She's been through a lot in the last few hours, he thought, better not to disturb her.

Paul leaned back and cradled the back of his head in his hands. And isn't this just great, he thought. There's a Hollywood starlet who wants to do it like a fish with me; there is no mother nor father looking to pounce on me for drinking beer and leaving the cans around the house, and, as a matter of fact, there is all the beer I'd ever want to drink in this camp—and yet all I have to do is get away from some crazy killer and this world and all that is in it will be mine.

Paul let his mind wander and thought about Cindy. Ha! Bet she was at the movies right now, munching on popcorn and totally enthralled in some passion play about young lawyers or young accountants or young congressional aides and the important decisions they have to face.

Adult Situations, Profanity, Nudity, Sex, Violence

Cripes, Paul thought. You want to know what real drama is like? You want to see a real four-star movie? Just look in a certain hay loft in a barn at a camp that just happens to have been overrun by a psychopath.

You'll find real drama there, for sure.

He wondered what Eddie and Phil were doing now. Probably telling each other how they got laid last night. Wish he could see them now. Cripes, would he love to tell them about Debi and the way she takes off her tube top.

Paul dozed, despite the promise he made to himself to stay awake. He didn't dream but woke suddenly and with a start. What was that? A noise? He crept slowly to the loft's overhang, then peaked over so he could see the barn door. The waxing gibbous moon was high in the night sky, sending steely white rays poking through the old slats of the barn roof. The white beams danced gingerly across the harsh wooden floor of the barn. There was that noise again. Definite movement. Was that a mouse scurrying across the floor?

Paul sidled back to Debi. He placed his hand over her mouth and shook her gently. She opened her eyes, slowly. In this loft, in this barn, under the moon's sharp albedo, Paul could tell they were Hollywood eyes.

"I think we better leave," he whispered.

Debi nodded, then rolled away from him and stood up. She started brushing straw from her clothes. Paul was about to tell her to stay in the shadows when he saw the hulking figure step forward into a square of light that was centered in the creaky barn floor.

Cripes, Paul thought.

He was tall, to be sure. And stocky with a weightlifter's arms and a linebacker's chest. He stared up at them through cruel, black eyes. He was dressed in a dark blue jogging suit that was liberally stained with blood. He wore a ski mask. He let an ax sway rhythmically by his side, gripping it loosely in rough, stubby fingers.

Paul felt the quiet; it was as if the night stopped turning into day.

And for a frozen moment, they regarded each other: looked one another over as if they had been sitting across the aisle on a subway train. The guy with the ax cocked his head to one side, then the other—as if he was waiting for a signal from Paul. As for Paul, he forgot his terror for a moment, wondering whether the dude would just walk away and leave them alone. Paul leaned back on his heels and decided that the hulking giant wanted him to show his fear. Paul suddenly decided not to. Paul knew he could be a cool dude; after all, be had a condom in his wallet, he was a badass bass player and he had a dozen empty beer cans under his front seat. Phil and Eddie would be dead by now. Even Steve with his perfect white teeth and his athletic good looks couldn't stare this guy down.

No, Steve and Eddie and Phil couldn't. But Paul could and Paul was doing it and Paul was still alive.

Yes, it was true. Cindy never understood him, never gave him a chance. He didn't care about her anymore, anyway. He knew he would never go back to her now, never again would he sit in the boring darkness at one of her crummy movies, never again would he put up with her crap in the backseat of the Chevy.

And never again would he steal condoms out of his father's bureau drawer. He was banging chicks like Debi now and they didn't care if he left the O in his wallet.

Paul was ready to shout to the creep: "Go away, asshole, I'm not afraid of you and your ax and your attitude. Just fuck off, man." All he had to do was show the man with the ax that he would feast on no fear in this barn tonight.

But Paul hadn't counted on Debi.

She broke the silence with a shriek. Cripes, Paul thought. The man with the ax looked up, hefting his weapon tightly in his hands. He crossed the floor in two strides and made it to the ladder of the hay loft. Paul backed away, glancing at Debi. She was screaming hysterically in short, staccato bursts.

The psychopath was in the loft now. He approached Debi, swung the ax once and neatly severed her head from her body. Her headless corpse collapsed in the loft, filling the dank barn air with a pink mist and soaking the hay with blood. Her head rolled to Paul's feet. coming to a rest face up. Her Hollywood eyes, once so blue and so sincere and so ready to love him were now sad and lifeless.

Paul turned and jumped out of the loft, then screamed out in agony when he hit the barn floor, breaking his leg. He looked up through his

Adult Situations, Profanity, Nudity, Sex, Violence

painful haze and saw the creepy dude hefting his huge body over the side of the loft and onto the ladder.

Paul started crawling across the floor of the barn, not really knowing what he was going to do next. He reached a corner of the barn and propped himself up on an elbow, then put his other hand up. The pain in his broken leg was nearly unbearable.

By now, the dude with the ax was standing over him.

Paul blinked through his fear. "Wait," he said. "I'm the last one alive, right? You can't kill me. At the end of all these movies, somebody is always left alive."

To Paul's amazement, the maniac stopped and spoke. "Yeah, you're right kid," he laughed.

Then he raised the ax.

"But this ain't the movies."

Tammy's Tips

Tammy stared at the screen of her computer. During the past hour, she had munched on an apple, smoked four cigarettes, drank a cup of coffee and then a Diet Pepsi. She bit her fingernails, too, but then noticed what she was doing and quickly stopped. She did, however, go to work on them with an emery board and thought briefly about applying a fresh coat of polish, but decided that she was too busy to do her nails. And besides, she wouldn't be able to type while waiting for the polish to dry.

Not that she had much to type, anyway. Tammy hadn't been able to write a word in three weeks. The third installment of *Tammy's Tips* was hardly more than a concept in the mind of Roger, her editor who had lately been pressing to see some sample chapters. Tammy had been able to hold Roger off with some vague excuses about research, but sooner or later she realized she was going to have to tell him that Tammy simply didn't have any more tips for him.

When the original *Tammy's Tips* hit the bookstores, it became an instant hit and spent four months on the bestseller lists. It was an alternate selection of the Book of the Month Club and made Tammy a national celebrity. She did the *Today* show and then *Good Morning America*. Oprah interviewed her. *Good Housekeeping* approached her about a regular column and there was even some talk about product endorsements and merchandising her name.

Tammy's tips were designed for working moms and other busy people who did not have time to spend in the kitchen or over a mop or on their knees scrubbing out an oven.

She would, for example, advise her readers to line the bottom of their ice cube trays with aluminum foil, which makes the ice pop out easily. Mirrors need cleaning? Tammy wrote that a balled-up newspaper page will put a squeaky shine on them. What to do with a load of clean clothes? Tammy advised her readers to always hang clean clothes in the back of their closets so every garment will receive an equal amount of wear.

She also had a somewhat homespun style of giving advice. "Always clean when you are angry at something. You'll find yourself more prone to picking up when all you really want to do is pick a fight," Tammy admonished on page 212 in the original *Tammy's Tips*.

Tammy followed up *Tammy's Tips* with *More Tips from Tammy*, which sold as well as the first book—well enough, in fact, to interest her publisher in a third volume. So, she collected a $100,000 advance and was given a deadline and the working title of *Still More Tips from Tammy*. And for the past three weeks she sat silently in front of her computer screen, haunted by a writer's block that was the mother of all writer's blocks.

The problem wasn't that she was out of tips. Tammy had notebooks full of ideas that she had been collecting since she was a kid. Her mother had died in childbirth and her father had been so distraught that he soon drank himself to death. She was raised by a grandmother, who worked as a maid cleaning middle-class homes. She often took Tammy along on the jobs and over the years passed down much of what she knew about cleaning houses to her granddaughter. Now, her grandmother lived in a condo in Redondo Beach, thanks in part to the more than 500,000 people who each shelled out $29.95 for *More Tips from Tammy*.

No, the problem wasn't a lack of tips. The problem was how to write about them. The first two books were really only a mishmash of helpful household hints with really no theme other than they would save you

Tammy's Tips

time. Tammy wanted the third book to be a bit more; perhaps it would have a theme, perhaps even a plot. Maybe, it would even tell a story, somehow. Trouble was, Tammy wasn't sure what she wanted to say, she only knew she didn't want it to be another version of the first two books. She thought about approaching Roger with the problem, but quickly discarded the idea. He would want the same old tips from Tammy. After all, why fool with success?

Jeff wasn't much help. Her husband was great at investing their money and making business decisions and booking her on talk shows, but he was totally useless when it came to literary advice. After *Tammy's Tips* was such a success, Jeff quit his job and went to work full time managing his wife's career. He picked out their new home in Bel Air, bought a black Corvette for himself and a white Corvette for her, invested their money in shopping centers in Michigan and negotiated her book deals. He seemed to live with his phone stuck in his ear.

"You worry about the words, I'll worry about the money," he would smile whenever Tammy would bring up the "theme" problem, as she came to call it. Tammy noticed that she and Jeff hardly ever talked anymore, except about business and books. He seemed to be consumed by their new fortune and was intent on promoting her into even bigger deals. Jeff was also big on publicity. He sent her out on radio, TV and newspaper interviews at least once or twice a week. They were a grind, and she was very thankful when he cut back on them so she could get down to work on the third volume. She hadn't been out on an interview in more than two weeks, although she seemed to recall one coming up.

As for Tammy, she really didn't have much interest in the business end. She didn't even know how much money they had, although she was certain it was in the millions by now. Not bad for a little girl raised by a housekeeper.

Despite everything, though, Tammy believed she was happy. Before the first book was published, there had been trouble in their marriage. She argued with Jeff a lot and they had even started talking about a separation. Tammy suspected him of cheating, but she couldn't prove anything. She was sad, lonely and unsure of her future. In fact, she wrote *Tammy's Tips* on the advice of a friend who was a professional family counselor. Her friend told her she needed a diversion from Jeff. So, she sat down and wrote the book in three months and sent it off to a publisher. She never expected it to sell; she had simply written it to take her mind off her marital troubles.

But then the letter of acceptance came and with it an advance for $10,000. And then came the bestseller lists and the Book of the Month Club and Kelly and Ryan and Oprah and the house in Bel Air and the Corvettes and everything else.

Jeff came into the room. He was on the phone, of course, apparently talking about an investment in a housing development in Oregon that he had mentioned to her a few days ago. Without breaking from his conversation, he walked over to Tammy and handed her a plane ticket. It was made out in her name. The flight was leaving that night for Colorado.

"What's this?" Tammy asked.

Jeff winked at her and kept talking.

She gave him a look of exasperation. "Well, what's this?"

"Hang on," Jeff said into the phone. Turning toward Tammy, he said, "You're doing *Good Morning, Denver* tomorrow. Surely you remember? It's a TV show in Denver. After the show you're going to sign some copies at the Barnes & Noble in downtown Denver."

Tammy sighed. She really didn't feel like going.

"They do the show live and it comes on at 6," Jeff continued. "That means you have to leave tonight. Better pack. I'll order an Uber for you in about an hour."

He turned away from her, lifted the receiver and went back to talking about the Oregon deal. Tammy shrugged. She hadn't remembered the Denver appearance was tomorrow, but that was not surprising. She hardly kept any of these appearances straight. She looked at the blank computer screen; at least she wouldn't be walking away from work. Tammy turned off the computer, packed her suitcase and waited for the Uber to arrive.

Her plane landed in Denver just past midnight. Tammy had never been a good airline passenger. She didn't find any of the in-flight entertainment of interest. She didn't feel like reading and found the meal to be quite indigestible. By the time she collected her luggage it was after 1 a.m. The TV station hadn't sent a limousine for her, which was usually customary. She tried calling the station and got no answer. Finally, she ordered an Uber but suddenly realized she didn't know where she was supposed to go. Usually, the TV station would put her

Tammy's Tips

up in a hotel the night before. She thought briefly about calling Jeff, but decided there was no sense waking him up and making him upset. She told the Uber driver to take her to the airport hotel. She spent a restless night.

The alarm went off at 5, rousing Tammy from a fitful sleep. She hardly felt rested and certainly didn't feel as though she could pull off the perky household helper act in only an hour from now. She tried calling the TV station again but still got no answer. Tammy checked out of the hotel, ordered an Uber and told the driver to take her to the station. About 45 minutes later the Uber arrived at the TV station where she immediately discovered a ring of union pickets surrounding the building.

The damned station was on strike? Well, that would explain why there was no limo at the airport and no answer at the station when she called. Of course, that meant there would be no show. Tammy smiled through it. The unexpected often happens, she told herself, and what could you do about it?

It was still early. Certainly, too early to go to the bookstore. She told the driver to take her to a good restaurant, where she had breakfast and sulked about *Still More Tips from Tammy*.

The theme, Tammy thought as she poked her eggs with her fork...the theme...the theme...the theme.

Maybe something about the environment? Recycling is big. Everybody wants to save the environment these days. Maybe I could just include tips that are environmentally safe.

Tammy wasn't in love with the idea. She looked at her cantaloupe and wondered why she had ordered it. She didn't like cantaloupe. Jeff liked cantaloupe; he always ordered it.

She heard a siren outside and glanced out the restaurant window next to her table. A fire truck sped by.

Maybe the theme could have something to do with saving lots of time. You know, it could be things you could do around the house in two minutes or less. Tammy smiled at the title: *Two-Minute Tips from Tammy*. Roger would love it.

Tammy wasn't sure she liked that idea either, but she decided to give it some more thought. Maybe Jeff could suggest something.

Ha! Mr. *I'll-Worry-About-The-Money* wouldn't be any help. All he cared about was making more money. Before the first book came out, he

203

didn't even care about her. She still wasn't convinced he cared about her now. She pushed her eggs with her fork and knew they were probably cold by now. She hated cold eggs.

Maybe the theme could be something sexy. That had promise. How to clean the house while wearing a lace teddy? Drive your man crazy? Do the dishes in crotchless panties?

Tammy threw her fork down, making a sharp clanking noise when it struck the porcelain plate. She wondered whether Jeff was playing house right now with some bimbo in a lace teddy. She found herself shivering with anger.

Tammy tossed some money onto the table and stalked out of the restaurant. It was just before 8 a.m. and the streets and sidewalks of downtown Denver were clogged with people and cars hurrying off to work. It was a busy time. Tammy really had no idea where she was or where she was walking. She vaguely remembered an appointment to sign copies at a Barnes & Noble, but she didn't really care about it now. She would divorce Jeff. He could have half the money, which is all he really loved anyway. She would start over and she knew she would be a success. After all, she was Tammy and she had her tips.

But she still didn't have a theme.

Just then another fire truck swept by her, its siren blaring. She screwed up her face against the blast of the siren and watched the truck swing around a corner. The noise shook her back to reality. The bookstore; she had a commitment to sign books. She ordered an Uber and gave the driver the address.

Ten minutes later the Uber was stopped by a traffic police officer as it approached an intersection near the bookstore. The cop told the driver that there was a fire on the next block and no traffic could get through. Tammy got out of the Uber and decided to walk to the bookstore. She wasn't sure how much business they were going to do or how many books she was going to sign with a big fire in the neighborhood, but Jeff had made the commitment and she aimed to keep it.

Well, the answer was no business and no books because it was the bookstore that was on fire. She stood watching the flames shoot out of the front of the store and the firemen scurrying around with their hoses and axes and air packs. She wondered how many of her books were going up in blazes inside the store. And then a policeman came up to her

Tammy's Tips

and asked her to step back and she wondered what kind of trip is it when the TV station goes out on strike and the bookstore burns down and you seriously entertain thoughts about divorcing your husband while your cantaloupe spoils and your eggs turn cold.

Divorce Jeff? Tammy laughed. Maybe she was just being foolish. Sure, he spent a lot of time counting her money but, after all, it had brought them together. Certainly, their marriage was in trouble before she became a best-selling author. Now that she had success, why shouldn't she share it with her husband?

Did he cheat? Tammy couldn't be sure. She decided to forget it for now. If she caught him at it, she would deal with it then. But until he slipped, why worry?

She looked at her watch. It was just before 9 a.m. She thought about calling Jeff and telling him about what had happened so far, but instead she decided to just find her way back to the airport. With any luck, she could be home that afternoon. And for once on this awful day her luck held out. The clerk at the ticket counter told her she was just in time for a flight back to Los Angeles, but she had to hurry. Tammy trotted to the departure gate and made it on board only minutes before the plane left.

She dozed on the flight back and didn't wake up until the 707 was slowing to a stop on the LAX tarmac. She awakened refreshed and not at all weary from the trip. She even had an idea for the theme: *Tammy's Tips for Travelers*. She would definitely talk to Roger about it.

As she walked through the LAX terminal she briefly thought about calling Jeff. Why bother? She'd be home in 45 minutes; way early, but there was nothing wrong so why bother him?

The traffic was surprisingly light by LA standards and her Uber moved quickly, weaving in and out of the freeway lanes. The driver was talkative and she found herself enjoying the friendly banter with him about the crooks in Washington, the bums at Dodger Stadium and the air pollution in Southern California.

It was a pleasantly warm day and Tammy felt comfort in the heat of the sun shining through the car windows. She couldn't wait to tell Jeff about how bollixed up the whole trip had been; she was sure they would enjoy a laugh over the whole thing. She was also bursting with ideas about *Tammy's Trips for Travelers*. Maybe her day in Denver hadn't been a failure after all.

And then she was home. She got out of the Uber and watched the car glide silently back toward the freeway. She turned and walked up the front steps, used her key and was inside the house.

She felt a chill. Something was not right. Tammy suddenly felt the urge to be silent. She resisted the temptation to call out Jeff's name; instead, she crept on little cat feet around the house, searching for… what? Evidence?

She stepped into the kitchen. The sink was piled high with dishes. It struck her that Jeff was a slob and had never read *Tammy's Tips*.

On the dining room table were two cocktail glasses. Both were empty. There was an open gin bottle on the table. Jeff never drank gin, he hated gin. Tammy fingered one of the glasses. It didn't look like any glass she owned. It had water spots on it, too. Tammy frowned. It definitely wasn't her glass—she knew how to get rid of water spots.

She put the glass back down on the table and crept upstairs. She walked silently, softly, toward the bedroom. The door was ajar. She placed her palm on it and pushed slowly…slowly…slowly. She peeked in. Jeff, her husband, was asleep in bed. A woman in his arms. Attractive, blond hair. Good figure. Who is it? Roger's wife, maybe. Tammy had met her at a party. She looked familiar. Was her name Sandy? No, Andie. Her name was Andrea, Roger called her Andie. Tammy didn't know too many people in Bel Air; it had to be Roger's wife. No matter. The woman was sleeping with Tammy's husband.

She had to die. Jeff had to die, too.

He kept a gun in the house. Where? His study. In a desk drawer. Tammy found herself in the study, unsure of how she got there. She didn't remember leaving the bedroom doorway, but here she was in Jeff's study going through the drawers of his desk. Here, in the top drawer, she found the gun. She picked it up and found herself back in the doorway of the room.

Tammy didn't know whether the gun was loaded; she wasn't even sure she knew how to use it. She pointed it at the woman, squeezed the trigger. Pop! The shot struck the woman in the forehead. She died in her sleep.

Jeff sat up. He was drunk, probably. Certainly, he was groggy, in a fog. He opened his eyes slowly and looked at Tammy. She squeezed off another round and struck her husband in the chest. He clapped his hand over his chest and watched the blood ooze out from the wound. Surprised, he looked back at his wife. Tammy fired again, striking Jeff in the neck. He coughed, then collapsed back and died.

Tammy stumbled out of the room and wandered around the house, sobbing quietly and unsure of what to do next. She found herself back in the study and sat down behind her late husband's desk. She laid the gun down on the soft green leather that stretched across the desk top. She picked up her phone and started dialing 911.

She stopped after the 9. No, she thought. They deserved to die. Certainly, Jeff did. And the woman was no better. Tammy saw no reason to call the police. "Why should I go to prison for a couple of cheaters?" She hung up the phone.

Now what? The bodies, she thought, I must get rid of the bodies. She jumped out of the seat and ran upstairs to the bedroom, bursting through the door. The scene brought her to a jolting stop. The bullet that struck Andie left a gaping hole in the woman's forehead. Blood had seeped out of the hole, and although the coagulation process had started, Andie's entire upper torso was covered in an oily slick of her own blood. The pillow was drenched, and so was the sheet under the corpse.

Andie was bad; Jeff was worse. His chest was now home to a red spider, its spiked legs shooting out from the epicenter of the wound. Jeff's half of the bed was awash in his own blood. But there was still more. She saw the neck wound and guessed her shot had severed his jugular vein. Jeff's lifeless head hung over the side of the mattress, a steady stream of blood still dripping through his scalp onto the shag carpet. It formed a red pool that seeped deep into the fabric; some of it had already dried, leaving a dirty brown stain.

Tammy stared at the scene.

"What a mess," she said.

* * *

Roger called a week later. Tammy was happy to hear from him.

"Good news," she told him. "The book is coming along great—I should be ready to email you some sample chapters any day."

"Terrific. I'm really anxious to see them."

They talked for a few minutes about the book and Roger said he loved her idea of giving it a theme.

"What do you have in mind?"

"I don't want to tell you yet, but I promise you'll love it."

Roger told her he was sure it would be a success.

"One other thing," he said. "My wife…Andie. Have you seen her lately?"

He told her that Andie hadn't been home in a week. Roger said he wasn't concerned about her, that he planned to leave her anyway because he was certain that she was seeing other men. Still, he wondered what she was up to now. Tammy said she hadn't seen Andie lately. Then she promised to get the chapters to Roger and hung up.

Tammy turned back to her laptop and read the title: *Tammy's Tips for the Toughest Jobs*.

She scrolled the screen until she reached the point where she had left off. The last paragraph she had written said: "Blood has always been a real tough stain. If you find it in your carpet, try to thin the stain first with ammonia and then. . ."

Tammy's Tips

To Control the Wolf

"You have a very common problem," Dr. Barnhardt told me in his squeaky voice as he leaned back in his chair. "I don't think your marriage is over, not by a long shot. I think with work, you and your wife can have a long and happy relationship."

I don't know whether I was relieved to hear that or not. I had agreed to see Dr. Barnhardt in a desperate effort to save my marriage and, quite frankly, I wasn't sure I was that interested in saving it. Still, there was something comforting in his words. I sat deep in the leather chair facing his imposing desk, surrounded by teak-paneled walls and framed degrees Dr. Barnhardt earned in psychology and couples therapy. A picture of Barnhardt and what I guessed to be his family stood on his desk. I suppose he had about a dozen kids.

He spoke again.

"You and Tess have a problem most young couples encounter soon after they start living together. Some of them are able to overcome it; some are not."

Well, he was right about our problem being common. Simply, we fought over everything. We fought over what to have for breakfast. We fought over balancing the checkbook. We fought over whether to visit in-laws. We fought over dents in the car. We fought over what to watch on TV. And we fought over everything else in between.

This had been going on for three years and I don't mind telling you I was ready to call it quits. But when Tess came to me with the idea of going to a couples therapy counselor, instead of fighting over it I told her it was OK, we should do it. I guess something deep inside me thought this marriage was worth saving, so for once I gave in. Maybe it was because I still felt an animal attraction to Tess.

She was a tall raven-haired beauty with an ample bosom and a dancer's legs. She exuded a certain dark sensuality; I was convinced she gave off an erotic scent that rose from deep within her sexuality.

There was a feral quality to our lovemaking—or, at least, there had been for a time. Now, it seemed as though our relationship was, at best, mechanical.

Anyway, I don't know how she found Dr. Barnhardt, but a week later she told me we had an appointment and that he charged $200 an hour.

So, we showed up in his office—after fighting over who would drive—and we sat in his waiting room for about 45 minutes and I kept an eye on his mousy red-headed receptionist whose nameplate said "Miss Tucker" and who seemed to be busy doing nothing, and then Dr. Barnhardt got on the intercom and told Miss Tucker to send in Tess, and then I sat for another half-hour wondering just what in the hell I was doing there.

When Tess came out Miss Tucker told me I could go in. I found Dr. Barnhardt to be a pleasant enough fellow; he jumped out from behind his desk to crank my hand when I walked into his office. He was short and roly-poly, balding, fifty-something and, I decided, probably a lot smarter than me.

He sat down and motioned me to sit, also. He put his elbows on his desk and smiled but said nothing for a few seconds. I felt foolish sitting there and was about to ask him what was going to happen next when he finally spoke.

"Did you ever wonder why some people never bother waiting in lines?" Barnhardt asked me. "Why they just walk right up to the ticket window at the theater, pushing in front of everybody else?"

"Huh?" was all I could think of saying.

To Control the Wolf

"Or why some people act like maniacs on the highway? Or why some people cheat on their income taxes? Or why some people have extra-marital affairs?"

I shrugged.

"It's the wolf within them," he explained. "You know, just like in the fairy tale—everyone has a little of the Big Bad Wolf inside them. Sometimes, the wolf shows himself. In the fairy tale, he terrorized the three little pigs. In real life, he drives like a maniac, cheats on his taxes and he won't wait in line at the theater."

I think I could see what he was saying.

"And the reason Tess and I fight a lot is because we each have the Big Bad Wolf inside us?"

Barnhardt smiled broadly and nodded his bald head vigorously.

"Right!" he declared.

"So…we have to learn how to control the wolf?"

He shook his head. "It's not that easy. That may be your problem and it may be more complicated than that. You see, I've only met you two today; I hardly know you. This was a good introductory session and I think you and your wife made a good start but I'd like to see you several more times before I'd be ready to declare your marriage secure. It may take a dozen more visits, maybe 20 or 30."

He had my attention with that one. At $200 an hour, this was going to get expensive.

I knew Tess would want to do whatever Barnhardt recommended. I could picture us fighting over it.

"But if we know what the problem is and we know we just have to control the, uhh, wolves inside us…why should it take such a long time? It seems to me to be a simple matter to just control our anger."

Barnhardt was playing with a pencil on his desk, tapping its eraser gently onto the soft green paper of his blotter.

"I'm not sure controlling the wolf is best for you," he said. "Some people need to let that wolf out—they try to contain it and sometimes the wolf just peaks out from time to time. Usually, when that happens they fight a lot with the people they know—often their spouses. I happen to know a lot of people who won't wait in line at the theater but they have very happy marriages. You see, it's a very complicated problem and I can't tell you the answer now. It's going to take many more sessions."

We chatted about the Big Bad Wolf for a few more minutes and then Dr. Barnhardt stood up and reached across the desk, giving me the signal that our session was over. I stood and shook his hand and left the office. On the way out, I gave Miss Tucker a check for $200 and she gave us another appointment for next week.

Tess and I had a strange relationship over the next few days. Both of us, I could tell, tried to keep the wolf inside, but it just didn't work. We still fought.

"You're the biggest slob in the world," she snapped at me one day, as she picked up my dirty socks from the floor.

"At least I don't leave wet stockings hanging over the bathtub," I snarled back. "That disgusts me."

Later, we decided to go see a movie but ended up fighting over what movie to choose. Instead, we stayed home—where we fought some more.

Our next session with Dr. Barnhardt finally arrived and, curiously, I found myself looking forward to it. Again, he took Tess first. I quickly became bored with the magazines in the waiting room and was forced to amuse myself by watching Miss Tucker munch on chocolates from a bowl on her desk. Finally, Tess emerged and I strode in to see Dr. Barnhardt.

"How's the wolf?" he asked, as I sat down.

I shrugged. "He showed up a number of times during the week. Tess's wolf showed up, too."

"I know," he answered. "She told me about it."

He asked me a lot of questions about my background during the rest of the session; about what I did for a living, about whether I was under stress at work, about my relationship with my parents and my brothers and sisters, and so on and so on. I answered all his questions truthfully and he made notes on his laptop. His little eyes sparkled throughout the session.

Obviously, he was trying to be as friendly as he could. I didn't think all those questions were accomplishing much, but I guess it was important for him to know about me. Still, when the session ended I felt as if it was all a waste of time. After all, couldn't I have just filled out a form and saved myself $200? I paid Miss Tucker on the way out and she gave us another appointment.

To Control the Wolf

We returned a week later and this time we really got down to business. Again, Tess went in first. While she was in with Dr. Barnhardt I thought I heard strange sounds, as if she was shouting and he was shouting; then I swore someone cried out in some kind of pain. I glanced over at Miss Tucker; she was working on a crossword puzzle. She looked up at me and smiled.

"What's a six-letter word for knot?" she asked.

I thought it over for a minute.

"Granny."

Miss Tucker popped her gum. "Thanks," she said.

I was so nervous I felt like a kid waiting to see the principal. When Tess emerged at last she appeared exhausted; it was clear that she was emotionally and even physically drained. Her face was flushed and her eyes were swollen—she had definitely been crying. Her clothes were even a bit disheveled. She plopped down in the chair next to me, closed her eyes and tilted her head back.

I went in.

Barnhardt had his jacket off. He sat with his sleeves rolled up, his tie loosened. An ash tray on his desk was overflowing with cigarette butts; in his left hand he held a fresh burning cigarette in his stubby fingers. His glasses were perched on the end of his nose. He leaned back and regarded me.

"How's the wolf?" he asked.

"Dunno," I mumbled.

He stubbed out the burning cigarette, then lit another. Barnhardt stared down at some papers on the desk in front of him. He seemed to be ignoring me. In fact, he swiveled his chair around so that he was no longer facing me. And that's how we sat there for something like 15 or 20 minutes. Occasionally, he would reach around to a pack of cigarettes on his desk. All I could think about was paying this guy $200 an hour so he could catch up on his reading.

I was getting madder and madder at the little bastard when he suddenly turned in his chair and faced me. "Tell me," he said, exhaling blue smoke, "what do you really hate about that bitch?"

I arched my eyebrows. Whom did he mean? My mother? My sister? Tess? Miss Tucker? Of course, I knew what he wanted me to say. I just didn't want to say it.

"Come on…what does that cow of a wife do that really busts your balls to no end?"

"Well," I said sheepishly, "I can't stand it when she takes one of her long bubble baths. She'll go into the bathroom, lock the door and will sit in the tub for an hour or more. We live in a small apartment and we have one bathroom, only. Sometimes, I have to take a piss but I have to hold it in until she finally comes out. I've told her about it and told her about it and she won't listen."

There, I thought, that was safe.

Barnhardt scowled at me. "Don't give me that crap. You should be able to hold in your piss for an hour. Now, let's have it. What does Tess do that just makes you want to smack her in the teeth?"

Geez, I was sweating under the collar. I was sweating in the armpits. I felt a bead of perspiration wind its way down my spine. My back hurt, my ribs hurt and my knees ached. I balled my hands into fists and felt the veins stretch out of my neck. This was going to be tough.

"I'll tell you," I growled. "I really can't stand it when that slut won't put out in bed…when she tells me she isn't in the mood. Man, I get so horny sometimes that I could rip her damn clothes off, but then she tells me to piss off and I just want to crack her across the jaw."

The words just came spilling out. I felt a renewed strength as I was saying them and as I was speaking I could feel the muscles in my chest puff up and my biceps expanding and my neck suddenly feel as though its sinews were made of steel cables. I roared out the words and let my tongue dance hungrily over my lips. "Yes!" I barked through my naked teeth and foul breath. "The next time she does that, I'm going to rip out her fucking throat!"

I then discovered that I was standing on the chair and for reasons that I couldn't explain, I had ripped my shirt open and had even scratched my fingernails across my chest. The scratches were bleeding, slightly. I also saw that I had been slobbering: I gave an embarrassed wipe across my mouth with my shirt sleeve. I suddenly felt dead tired. Exhausted, I collapsed in the chair and heaved for air.

Barnhardt smiled.

"See you next week," he said.

* * *

To Control the Wolf

Tess and I rode home in silence. We had little to say to each other for the rest of the day, even at dinner. Finally, the day came to an end and we went to bed. Just then it started to rain and the pitter-patter of the rain against the bedroom window made it difficult to sleep. I tossed about in bed for a bit, then got up for a drink of water. It was after 2 a.m. and I wasn't a bit tired. Instead, I was edgy...nervous for some reason. I felt caged. By now the rain had stopped. A walk, I concluded, would make me feel better. I don't know what made me decide on that. I'm not the type of person who gets out of bed at 2 a.m. and goes for walks. Still, I found the urge hard to resist. I dressed quickly and quietly and left our apartment building.

It felt good to be out in the cool night air. The waning crescent moon was high in the sky, casting its reflection in the puddles left over from the storm. The streets were devoid of traffic; the sidewalks, likewise, were empty. It was a special time of the night, a time to be free and unchained. I walked briskly, feeling strangely exhilarated. I picked up the pace and even started to jog. Finally, I let it all loose and broke into a run. I wondered how long I could keep it up. After all, I'm not really an athletic person.

Nevertheless, I just felt like running and running and running as fast as I could. The wind smacked me in the face. I splashed through a puddle and felt the water saturate my clothes. I laughed and somehow found the strength to pick up the pace even more. I came to a traffic barrier with a sign on it that said the road ahead was closed. I leaped over it without breaking stride, then kept on running. Ahead of me was a ditch, perhaps 10 feet wide. No problem for me—I jumped and made it across easily, then kept on running.

I approached an all-night diner. I slowed my pace and trotted by. A lone customer was seated at the counter. In front of him, a cook was broiling a hamburger. Something stirred in the pit of my belly: I felt hungry...ravished, in fact. I suddenly had the urge to break in through the window of the diner. I really wanted to taste that red meat that was sizzling away only a few feet away from me. Maybe, even, bite into something a bit more, well, a bit more raw.

I backed up a few steps to get a running jump at the window and then...

I stopped myself.

What am I doing?

Control yourself, I told myself.

Control yourself.

Control yourself.

Control the wolf.

And then a car turned the corner. It was a police cruiser. I growled, then ducked into the shadows. The squad car parked in front of the diner. The cop got out and went in. I crept away; when I was certain I was out of sight of the diner I started running again.

I don't know how much longer I ran—maybe 10 minutes, maybe 15 minutes. Finally, I stopped. I panted for air and sat on the curb to rest. And then I noticed a few things about myself. For instance, somewhere along the way I had lost my shoes and socks. My clothes were tattered. Also, I was terribly lost. I had run so far and for so long that I had run myself right out of my neighborhood. How could I get home? I stood and, suddenly, my nose twitched. Something…some type of odor…told me how to get home. Call me crazy, but that's how I found my way home.

After walking for about an hour I came to our apartment complex. I approached our building and saw the front door was wide open. Did I leave it that way? I didn't think so. Burglars? Was Tess OK? I approached the building slowly, then slipped inside. Our apartment is on the second floor. Rather than ride up in the elevator I took the stairs, creeping up the steps as silently as I could. Once on the second floor I looked down the hallway and saw our apartment door was open as well. Had I left that door open? I entered our apartment and switched on the lights. Everything seemed to be in order. I must have left the door open, after all. Suddenly, I realized how exhausted I was. See, I told myself, that walk outside had helped.

I changed back into my pajamas and then noticed for the first time that Tess wasn't in bed. Maybe she's in the bathroom.

"Tess!" I called out. "Tess, are you here?"

No answer.

Strange.

I shrugged, crawled into bed and quickly fell asleep.

The next morning I woke up and found Tess in bed next to me. She didn't tell me where she had been and I didn't ask.

To Control the Wolf

* * *

Later that day I was sitting in my desk at home balancing the checkbook when I noticed the number on the next check didn't match up with the last number in the check register. I shook my head. Tess, again. She had a habit of writing checks and not recording them, which really fouled up the bookkeeping. It also meant we occasionally bounced checks, because neither she nor I had any idea of the balance in the checking account.

"Tess!" I shouted. "Get in here!"

She came striding over a minute later. She frowned. "What now?"

I waved the checkbook at Tess and told her that she hadn't been recording the checks again. "So, what?" she hissed at me. "You'll figure it out."

I threw the checkbook at her; then I stood and smacked her across the teeth with the back of my hand. I was shocked: throughout all our troubles, I had never once hit her. I was mulling this over in my mind when she turned back to me and suddenly raked her nails across my face.

I howled in pain and brought my hands up to my face. I was bleeding a bit. But I noticed something weird. The blood, on my hands…it tasted, well, sort of…good.

Before I could give any more thought to this notion Tess suddenly punched me in the stomach and I doubled over—a bit surprised at her strength. I glanced up and saw her coming at me again, smiling broadly and baring her teeth. This time I was faster than she was. I easily dodged her lunge and caught her in the back of her head with my fist. She hit the top of the desk hard and shrieked in pain. I didn't give her a chance to come back at me. I yanked on her hair and pulled her toward me, snarling as I ripped the blouse from her body and sank my pointed teeth in the back of her neck. I tasted her blood and hungrily slurped at it with my long, wet tongue.

She arched her back and let out a grunt, then spun and clawed at my ears. I couldn't believe how fast she moved. Her snout was dribbling puss and her fangs were bare. She barked in my face, then clawed at my eyes. I barked back.

We wrestled for a few minutes, neither of us gaining the advantage. Finally, she weakened a bit and I moved in. I bit furiously at her neck while she howled in anguish. I tasted the matted fur below her jaw and was ready for the kill when she somehow found a new reservoir of strength and pushed me away. I was startled, but instinctively I knew she would be coming for me so I readied myself for the next assault.

Tess climbed onto the desk and with incredible strength launched herself at me, hurtling across the room and knocking me over. We were both stunned by the impact, and as we locked again in struggle and pushed and pulled against each other, I felt my strength leaving me. A sense of horror crossed through my mind as I imagined the battle coming to an end and no way to defend myself. But Tess was weakening, too. We both made attempts to hurt each other, to bite and scratch and paw, but soon we collapsed in each other's arms. Exhausted, we fell asleep.

When I awoke hours later I looked at my wife and saw her eyes slowly opening, too. We were still very much entwined in each other's bodies. Our clothes were in shreds, we were bloodied, beaten and grimy. It seemed as if every muscle in my body ached. The apartment looked as if it had been hit by a missile.

"Wow," Tess giggled.

And then we had the greatest sex of our marriage.

* * *

Our next appointment with Dr. Barnhardt was late Friday afternoon. We were the last patients in the waiting room when he got on his intercom and told Miss Tucker that both Tess and I should come in together.

"And you can go now," he told his receptionist. "This is my last appointment. I'll lock up."

Tess and I were a little surprised to be going in together. We rose, and as we did Miss Tucker also got up. She put on her coat and left the office.

Tess and I sat down in front of Dr. Barnhardt's desk. He looked coldly at us. "Before we begin today, I think you better explain something to me."

He held up three checks. They were the payments I had given Miss Tucker for the first three visits. Barnhardt frowned. "Each one of these checks bounced," he complained, shaking the checks back and forth. He was quite angry.

To Control the Wolf

"OK...OK...OK," I told him. "Don't get excited. I'll make out new ones for you."

"Well, you better," Barnhardt spat back at me. "After all I've done for you two, and this is how you repay me? I'm putting a lot of kids through college and I can't afford to carry deadbeats in my practice. This hour can be used by paying clients, you know."

"Listen you little pig!" I shouted back at him. "I said I'd pay you. Now cool off, will you?"

"Don't tell me to cool off," he screamed back. And then little roly-poly Dr. Barnhardt with the squeaky voice let out a series of cuss words that would make a sailor blush. As he was shouting at us, I looked at Tess and Tess looked at me and, well, we both bared our teeth.

* * *

Miss Tucker found what was left of Dr. Barnhardt early Monday morning. His head had been neatly severed from his body. An arm was over in a corner of his office; it had teeth marks on the bloody stump of bone that poked through the rotting flesh. There was a deep gash in his chest cavity and his heart was missing—it was as if someone with incredible strength simply reached in and yanked it out. Nobody could find it, either.

His carpet was ruined by the oily slick of blood that pooled under the corpse. Most of the framed degrees had been ripped off the walls and torn to shreds.

The medical examiner wrote in his report that Dr. Barnhardt died from an attack committed by some type of wild animal, most likely a wolf. One expert called to the scene even guessed that it was the work of two wolves.

The police were baffled.

Too bad about Dr. Barnhardt. He sure saved our marriage.

The Spider's Protocol

Here are the first four chapters of an unpublished novel titled The Spider's Protocol, a surreal tale of an ordinary house spider and the unusual charcters who stop by his web for a chat.

Ozzie

I caught a fly in the web the other day.

Miserable beasts, flies. Terrible B.O. I think it comes from buzzing around shit all day. Especially dog shit.

And stupid, too.

Anyway, he tells me his name is Ozzie and he snuck into the house through a hole in the screen. He thinks he's oh-so-clever. He says the people who own the house don't know they have a hole in the screen, and that's how he got in. Ozzie says he expects a lot of flies will enter that way.

He laughs at this.

So do I.

I didn't get in the house that way. I was born here. I hatched out of an egg not too far from where my web is today. I had something like a hundred-fifty brothers and sisters, and about a third of us escaped before Mom ate the rest. That's protocol with spiders: they eat their young.

My earliest memory is running for my life. The egg broke open; that much I remember. I pushed away the creamy shell, using each of my eight legs, and thinking back on that day I can tell you it was not unlike the way a baby chicken breaks out of a shell. There was a lot of shoving and cracking and peeling back the shiny glutinous blanket and, finally, I was out.

I took a deep breath. The air smelled dank. I tried to focus my eight eyes, but I could see little. My vision is as poor today as it was on the day of my birth. I can see images and shapes, but I have trouble focusing.

I saw a large black blur coming my way. It had a familiar smell—more or less like the silk sac that held my egg only a few moments ago. The image grew larger as the blur came closer.

"Mommy?" I asked.

The beast continued to bear down on me. As she drew closer she said, "Hello...my little Honeybunch."

Honeybunch?

Well, bullshit on that. Instinct told me to get the hell out of there. I started running, looking over a few of my shoulders, and all around me my brothers and sisters were running as well. I stepped over them; I stepped over eggs; I stepped over cold, damp concrete that made up the basement floor. Around me was darkness; I guess my birth must have come at night.

Run faster, I told myself. Faster, faster, faster. Behind me, I could smell the cool evil breath of my mother. She was gaining on me. I was just a little baby spiderling at the time, while my mother was a full-grown beastly arachnid.

Eight long, hairy legs, trampling over her own eggs, her own children. My mother picked up my scent and bore down on me, baring her slimy fangs. I still shudder to think about it.

And then she made her move. She lunged; I darted to the right, narrowly evading her grasp. (Mom may have been big, nasty and evil, but she was a bit of a klutz.) Instead, she speared one of my sisters—I think it was Sue Ellen—and then she scooped her up and with one crack of her jaws tore Sue Ellen in half.

The Spider's Protocol

I was sprayed with Sue Ellen's juices. Although the aroma told me the liquid was sweet, and although I was beginning to feel the first real pangs of spider hunger, I was too terrified to stop and lick Sue Ellen's blood off myself.

I glanced over my shoulder one last time and saw my sister devoured by Mom. Then, I noticed some shadows over in the corner of the basement right by the French drain and made for them. By the time Mom was finished eating Sue Ellen I was safe.

I gasped hard and tried to catch my breath.

"Cripes!" I thought to myself. "What kind of world is this?"

I don't know how long I remained in the French drain. It could have been minutes, hours, whatever.

Soon, my fear gave way to hunger. To survive, I would have to eat. To eat, I would have to use my inherent spider craftiness as well as the tools nature had provided me. In other words, I would need a web.

I looked around for a place to spin my own web.

Thinking back on that experience, it was a frightful yet dizzying and almost exhilarating time in my life. Every spiderling goes through it, and those of us who survive the ordeal appreciate those early minutes of our lives as a sort of spider's boot camp under fire. Funny, but I find myself looking back on those days with a certain fondness. Of course, I don't waste my time telling Ozzie any of this.

Ozzie, I couldn't care less about.

I gasp as I breathe in the miserable fly's B.O. and then I suck out his juices. Ycccchh. Flies not only smell bad and are stupid, but they taste terrible.

Well, at least it's dinner.

Spiders Die Because They Don't Know How to Live

So, there I am, gasping for breath in the French drain and my mother the cannibal is still eating my brothers and sisters. She is insatiable. I see so much carnage that day it really does a lot to sour me on life in general. That's why I can eat a poor slob like Ozzie and not feel anything for the guy. That's right, nothing. No remorse, no thought about his family, no sudden sense of shame at all.

Soon, daylight creeps in through the window well of the basement. I'm hungry, but what can I do? Mom isn't exactly in the mood for breast-feeding at this point, eh?

As I said, I estimate that maybe a third of the spiderlings from Mom's brood have hatched and have gotten away. That means there are about fifty baby spiders hiding around the basement in various corners and crevices. My guess is another thirty-five or forty of us will die in the next few hours, mostly from starvation. Maybe some of us will be caught by Mom or even other adult spiders, maybe some of us will find ourselves crushed underfoot when some snot-nosed brat comes down the stairs looking for his baseball. And maybe some of us will die because we just don't know how to live. Mostly, though, I expect most of us will die from starvation.

But some of us will survive.

I look around the French drain. Suddenly, I see a flea. Little fellow. Must be a cat or a dog upstairs and this guy decided to jump off and take a rest.

I sidle up to him and tell him I'm new in town. He tells me to watch my ass, there's a big nasty spider around somewhere.

I thank him for the advice. "No sweat," he says.

Cripes, I think, as I sink my fangs into the bastard, fleas are dumb as dirt. Here I am, barely a few minutes old, and I've already outsmarted the asshole.

Cripes.

Sex the Dipteran Way

I find myself thinking a lot about webs lately.

They are marvels of natural engineering, particularly the orb webs that are composed of concentric circles which are then connected together by radial lines.

Webs are what we use to snare our prey. They are unabashed traps, made up of sticky viscous threads. A fly comes along and lands and he's mine.

Chomp!

The Spider's Protocol

And yet, we don't try to camouflage our work. There is nothing about a spider's web to make you think it is anything other than a spider's web. Its purpose is to catch something to eat, and it is out there in all its naked intent for the entire entomological community to gaze upon. True, we spiders often hide off to the side—appearing on the scene only when we have snared our dinner. That's the spider's protocol. Yet, again, if anyone came along and asked me why I'm so busy spinning a sticky silk parachute out of thread that seemingly comes out of my ass, I would tell him it's so I can catch bugs to eat. No foolin' about that on my part.

But nobody ever asks. Take Ozzie, for example. He came buzzing down the basement the other day and I watched him for hours. He flew by my web dozens of times. He had to see what I was up to. Finally, he lighted a few inches from the web, and then he slowly crept over and soon found himself tangled in the sticky silk of my orb web.

I approach Ozzie, ready to suck out his juices, but before I can do that he says hi and tells me his name is Ozzie and then he sort of just makes conversation. And does he ever talk! He tells me all about his day, about how he copulated that morning with a dipteron named Liz; how he ate some dog shit then flew into the house through the hole in the screen; how he buzzed around for a few minutes then landed on some kid's bowl of cereal (he really laughs at this); how he very nearly got swatted flat while resting on the oven door; how he ducked down the basement but couldn't find his way back upstairs, and how glad he is that he met me because I look like a nice fellow and wouldn't I be a sport and tell him how to find the kitchen because he still has somedog shit on his feet and he wants to land on somebody else's breakfast.

"I hope they're still eating upstairs," he chuckles.

I tell him I hope they are, too. And then he laughs some more.

"You're a good guy," he says. "When I figure out how to get back upstairs, I'll find my way out of the house and then I'll see if I can find Liz and I'll see if she has a sister for you. Would you like that, fella? Would you like me to fix you up with a horny dipteran?"

Ozzie pauses and stares at me for an instant, a sincere look of bafflement crossing his mandibles. At first, I think he's finally figured out that I plan to eat his innards, but then he breaks into a wide smile. I think he has formed a mental image of me and Liz's sister having sex the dipteran way. This makes him laugh some more.

227

Ozzie has a high, squeaky, moronic laugh which, I can tell you, is common in your ordinary housefly. But I like his laugh. It amuses me.

While Ozzie is telling me all about his life and laughing at his own jokes he's trying to untangle himself from the web. Not once does he ask me whether it's my web and if it is could I please help him get untangled. He sort of just keeps struggling and pulling and wrapping himself up tighter. Finally, the poor bastard exhausts himself and stops struggling. But he never stops talking.

"So, then I tell Liz that she was the best lay I ever had, and don't you know but the stupid broad believes me, and she says that if our little act of nooky out in the dandelions results in a brood of baby flies she'll be sure to name one of them Ozzie, and I say that would be really nice of you to do that, Liz."

And then he sort of furrows his compound eyes. "Between you and me what do I care about that because I've been with a hundred broads most of them classier than Liz and a lot better lookin', too, and maybe there are fifty or sixty little Ozzies buzzing around outside, and not only that but Liz wasn't such a good lay, after all."

He turns away from me and pulls at the silk and then he tries to push it away, but this just gets him tangled up more than he already is. None of this seems to bother him. He just laughs some more.

"Yeah," he says. "Liz was OK, but I've had better."

I've heard enough. Ozzie is a nice enough guy—as flies go—and I have enjoyed his company, but I am hungry so I sink a fang into Ozzie, giving him a generous dose of venom, and then I start slurping my supper.

The last look I remember Ozzie giving me is one of sincere and genuine puzzlement. Even through his compound eye, I can tell he's confused as all hell.

Shameless Self-Promotion

My first molt.
Let me tell you about it.
It's really a coming-of-age ordeal for the spiderling. Well, at least it was for me.

The Spider's Protocol

I think I was more than a few days old; certainly, not more than a week. Anyway, I woke up one morning feeling like shit. I had spun a little web—my first—and although I hadn't yet caught anything I was perfectly content to hang upside down waiting for Victim No.1.

But on this particular morning, every muscle in my cephalothorax felt as though it would burst.

I'm sure you can understand that feeling.

As the morning moved on, I found my appetite waning. My desire to hunt left me. All I wanted to do was hang upside down and hide in the shadows of the basement. A small tumblebug scurried across the floor right in front of my web. I could have leapt off the gossamer and had him in an instant, but I just shrugged and sort of waved my third leg on the left side. I meant it merely as a half-hearted show of conciliation—that I wanted him to know it was OK with me if I didn't eat him—but I don't think he ever noticed. He just ran by, then jumped into the French drain and I never saw him again.

The miasma grew worse. I felt my heart racing, my blood pumping faster. Fear overtaking me. I wondered whether I was going to die, and then I found myself thinking that it really didn't matter.

I might have dozed during that period, I don't know. Certainly, my thoughts weren't coherent. I remember my mind dancing from thought to thought—memories of my birth, of my mother eating her brood, of my sister Sue Ellen crushed to death by my mother's jaws, of that first flea I ate, of my hours in cold, damp corners of the basement.

And then, I noticed the physical differences. Oddly, my hindquarters started shrinking. I noticed my new consistency—I felt thin and brittle and not very comfortable, and I very much wanted to be rid of this uncomfortable, unseemly, unsettling feeling.

And then my ass tore open. That's right, my ass tore open. As you can imagine, that really shocked me. Here I am, a young spiderling, and I can't explain to myself what's happening to me nor can I understand the changes my body is going through. But as I gazed upon myself, I saw my wretchedly brittle skin tearing apart and flaking off my body.

And then, as I puzzled over this physical change, I suddenly found a new strength. I discovered that if I expanded my chest, the tearing and flaking was enhanced. So I sucked in a great gust of air and held it there while the thin exoskeleton that had covered me since my birth ripped and tore and fell away from my body in silly little flakes. There was no pain involved here; instead, as I discarded each shard of useless exoskeleton my vigor found renewal. New energy coursed through my body.

Finally, I jumped off my web and landed four-square on my eight legs. I arched my back and lifted my front two legs in a defiant, defensive posture. I intended it to be a challenge to the world. Or, at least, to the basement.

"Here I am!" I shouted. "Fuck with me and I'll shit silk all over you! I'll grind you in my jaws and suck your life's blood from your guts! You stupid smart-ass bugs don't stand a chance around me. I'm a grown-up spider now, so watch your little bug asses."

I don't know if anybody heard me or if anybody was really paying attention, but that sort of self-congratulation is important to spiders. Being solitary types, we don't exactly travel with a herd of sycophants cheering us on. So, we have to act as our own cheerleaders. I bet you didn't know that about spiders, but I can assure you that shameless self-promotion is a big part of the spider's protocol.

Anyway, the last bits of exoskeleton flew off my back. The molting process had been completed. There would be other molts to come, to be sure, but the first molt is always the molt you remember the most.

I was no longer a spiderling. I wasn't yet an adult but I was larger now and stronger as well. My senses seemed keener, although my eyesight remained poor as ever. Still, I looked back at my former spiderling web and found myself disgusted at its puniness. I would need a new web. Soon, I would get down to work.

But first, I gazed upon myself and regarded what nature had provided. And I was more delighted to be a spider at that moment than at any other time in my life.

The Spider's Protocol

Photo Credits

Photos and illustrations that appear in this book were drawn from public domain sources. They include:

Pixabay.com, pages 3, 4, 20, 96, 182, 198 and 222.

Free-Images.com, pages 6, 30, 34, 50, 64, 68, 76, 100, 104 and 181.

US Library of Congress, pages 10, 24, 46, 146, 150, 158 and 178.

Unsplash.com, page 38.

Gutenberg.org, pages 82 and 162.

Pickpik.com, page 209.

WikiArt.org, page 210.

Wikimedia Commons, pages 108, 116 and 168.

National Library of Spain, page 174.

The photos and images that appear on pages 56, 88, 112, 120, 124, 128, 134, 136, 142, 166 and 231 are by the author.

About the Author

Hal Marcovitz worked in the daily press from 1976 through 2006 as a reporter and columnist. He is the author of more than 200 nonfiction books for young readers. He has published short stories and the novel *Painting the White House*. He is the co-author of *Notes on Bucks County*, which describes the political evolution of Bucks County, Pennsylvania. You can find out more about Hal and his work by visiting his website, paintingthewhitehouse.com.

www.ingramcontent.com/pod-product-compliance
Lightning Source LLC
LaVergne TN
LVHW010316070526
838199LV00065B/5583